The Cowboy Says I Do

The Cowboy Says I Do

A Montana Rodeo Brides Romance

Sinclair Jayne

The Cowboy Says I Do
Copyright © 2021 Sinclair Jayne
Tule Publishing First Printing, August 2021

The Tule Publishing, Inc.

ALL RIGHTS RESERVED

First Publication by Tule Publishing 2021

Cover design by Lynn Andreozzi

No part of this book may be used or reproduced in any manner whatsoever without written permission except in the case of brief quotations embodied in critical articles and reviews.

This is a work of fiction. Names, characters, places, and incidents are products of the author's imagination or are used fictitiously. Any resemblance to actual events, locales, organizations, or persons, living or dead, is entirely coincidental.

ISBN: 978-1-954894-13-6

Dedication

I want to thank Tule—Jane, Meghan, Nikki and Cyndi—for green lighting the series. It started as a what if challenge on a phone conversation with Jane Porter, fierce and fearless Tule leader and so much more. Jane has been a friend for many years. She always listens and encourages and forces me to dig deeper and reach higher. The series evolved on the Oregon Coast on a writing retreat with my friend, Rusty Keller, in mid-March 2020 just as the world was prepping to shut down. Thank you Rusty for listening, asking questions, and reading my proposal drafts. A huge thank you to my editor Julie Sturgeon. It was not my intention, but she really had to work hard on this project as the three stories happen concurrently and the premise had a tendency to run away from me at times. Julie never seemed frustrated, but I imagined hearing an eye roll or two even across the Continental Divide.

Hope you enjoy,
Sinclair Jayne

Dear Readers,

I love writing cowboy stories. So iconic. So fun. The men have their own rules, ooze confidence and action is their language. So, I can't help wanting to mess with their heads just a little bit—stir them up, throw them off their game. This vision and desire—to throw something new into the cowboy mix started at my niece's wedding three years ago. My husband of twenty plus years is originally from India, and my talented sister-in-law knows how to throw a gorgeous, slap down party so when her only daughter got married, it was three days of food, family, friends and celebrating. We took over a hotel in Charlotte, and the wedding was flawlessly fun and elegant to the point that I felt like I'd walked into a reality show.

The prologue in *The Cowboy Says I Do*, is what sparked my idea of the Montana Rodeo Brides series. At my niece's wedding, all the women, swimming in vibrant color burst out of the hotel lobby to meet the groom—on a horse—with his entourage surrounding him. Bhangra music blared from the back of a truck leading the way down the street and into the hotel parking lot. We began dancing and laughing and everyone talking at once. My teen daughter was wearing a beautiful saffron salwar kameez that my friend, Mary Krummel had sewn for her from fabric I'd ordered online. We were spinning around looking at how the sun shone through the different fabrics of the scarves and skirts—

saffron, magenta, teal, and I wanted to capture the visual beauty and movement along with the sense of beginning and an ending of sorts. Hope, love and adventure imbued that day. But I still felt a pang of loss of the little girl I'd watched grow up into a beautiful, accomplished and confident woman waiting to start her new life in a new home.

As our world started shutting down and my college-age son had to come home and my daughter's high school senior year was cut brutally short in March 2020, I missed our family in North Carolina more and more as we could no longer visit. I started brainstorming a new series to write. I'd wanted to include a piece of my husband's and children's heritage. Even though I couldn't visit my family, I could have them with me in a story. My first East Indian-American heroine was born. And then I gave her a cowboy to love.

Prologue

With the bhangra music blaring from the back of the bright red Ford F-150 truck that was starting to lead the procession of men on a slow wind through the Denver hotel's parking lot, Ashni Singh made a final adjustment on her cousin Reeva's bloodred sari.

"Sure you want to go through with this?" she teased, barely keeping her voice grave, even after her years of performing in high school and college musicals.

"You have a better idea?" Reeva played along like she always had.

"There's this new rooftop bar that just opened up on California Street. They have a specialty cocktail with the word orgasm in it."

"Shshshsh" Reeva bit off a shocked giggle and hip-checked her. They both smiled at the collection of aunties pressing their noses against the double glass doors waiting for their cue to spill out to greet the approaching groom, groomsmen and men attending the afternoon wedding. Reeva's mom was reminding everyone about what to do, as if they hadn't all done this dozens of times before for different brides and different grooms.

But now it was Reeva's turn, and Ash wanted the day to be perfect.

"The aunties are definitely misbehaving." Ashni flipped her scarf gracefully back over her shoulder. "They were rating John's friends, especially Caleb."

"He is ratable." Reeva looked at her, a bit more calculation in her expression. "With the kilt, his muscular calves are totally on display, and he's very single."

"I'm not." Ashni felt her mood dip despite her determination to ignore the expected but hurtful barrage of questions lobbed her way the past couple of weeks. The main one—when was she going to get married? She'd just turned twenty-nine, and the reminders that she was "nearing the end of her shelf life," had been anything but subtle.

"You are tonight." Reeva winked. "Walk on the wild side, flirt a little, dance, maybe sneak a kiss. You've never even kissed any other guy except Beckett."

Whereas Reeva had happily dated in high school and college and after, sharing many of her adventures over coffee or cocktails or FaceTime, Ashni had left Denver to work in the marketing department for the pro rodeo tour to be closer to her long-time boyfriend and one of the tour's stars. Then Reeva had met John on a dating app, five months after finishing dental school and getting a job in a thriving downtown practice. She'd called Ashni in the middle of the night after her first date with John. She'd met the one. Six months later they were marrying.

And Ashni, who'd fallen in love with Beckett Ballantyne

in high school, was still unmarried.

"I don't tell if you kiss." As Reeva turned the words of the familiar phrase around, her beautiful dark eyes heavily lined with black eyeliner and dusted with gold, shone with happiness and mischief.

"Just as your secrets are safe with me." Ashni pulled Reeva into a hard hug.

This was it. Her best friend and cousin was getting married. Her life would be with John now. Her happiness and sorrows would first be shared with him. Ashni felt as if something inside of her ripped wide open, and a cold wind blew through.

"I'm so happy for you." She meant it to the marrow of her bones.

"Before this time next year, you'll be married too. I know it," Reeva hugged her back. "And we'll both be knocked up and the aunties will complain that we're gaining too much weight even as they shove food at us and remind us that we need to eat for two."

A wave of dread swept over Ashni so fast she feared she'd drop to her knees and pull Reeva down with her. This was Reeva's weekend. Her wedding. Her moment. And Ashni would never let the hurt that had been building since last Christmas interfere with a molecule of her cousin's happiness.

She could hear the song "Dholna" kick on as the truck made the first turn in the parking lot—a large group of men dancing behind and John festively regal in a *sherwani* and a turban, riding on a decorated horse, surrounded by his male friends and family in suits—Caleb, always original in a kilt—all dancing.

Ashni dropped a kiss on Reeva's sleek head—her beautiful blue-black hair was twisted elaborately into a low updo threaded with pearls and gold.

"No turning back now."

"Don't want to," Reeva said, her eyes shining more beautifully than diamonds.

"Let's dance," Ashni sang out in her best David Bowie impersonation. She linked arms with Reeva and pulled her into the center of the vibrantly colorful women—family and friends—as they spilled out into the beautiful, sun-drenched Denver afternoon.

As Ashni spun in a circle, she easily incorporated a few of the popular moves in the newer Bollywood movies into some of the traditional dances she and so many of her cousins had studied growing up in their *Shastriya Devesh* weekend dance school. She twirled and sang and reached her arms up gracefully—her fingers, dance moves, and facial expressions told the story of love. She watched the flare of the saffron skirt of her *lehenga* as she danced to celebrate Reeva and love and Reeva and John's sparkling future.

And she hated that even surrounded by so much joy and family and friends, she'd never felt more alone.

Chapter One

"There you are, cowboy," his cousin Bodhi Ballantyne greeted him at the large sponsor tent where Beckett Ballantyne had been signing autographs and posing for pictures before the Panhandle Rodeo finals started. A few carnival-style games had been set up outside the tent along with a roping demonstration.

Beck waved at the family he'd been posing with and checked his watch. He'd stayed fifteen minutes past his volunteer slot, and since another couple of rodeo cowboys had arrived, he thanked the coordination volunteers and stepped over the low white picket fence with fake floral arrangements and hay bales that had been set up for the family photos with the cowboy of their choice.

"I raised nearly twenty-five hundred dollars for the children's hospital in Boise," Beck said happily.

"I raised nearly three thousand yesterday." Bodhi didn't miss a beat. He never did.

"Seriously?" Beck's disappointment stabbed deep even as his competitive spirit flared. "My line was the longest they had today, and the volunteers asked if I could come back after my final events."

"Won't nobody be there…" Bodhi's amused glance raked over him as they exited the tent "…seeing as everyone with a pulse will be watching me ride Victory to a truly devastating first place in the bull-riding finals. That one hundred percenter rank bull is gonna lose."

"Bowen won't let you squeak out another win over him that quick." Beck laughed. "He drew Head Banger, who's scored more performance points than Victory on his last four rides."

"Exactly. You boys done discussing my superiority and ready to redeem yourselves?" Bowen Ballantyne, his cousin who was older by almost three years that had felt like a decade when Beck had been a kid trying to keep up, sauntered over, carnival game tickets dangling from his fingers. "Who's willing to accept the challenge?"

Bodhi snatched the tickets. Beck immediately swiped them away.

"Ever heard of sharing?" Bowen produced another wad of tickets that he tossed at Bodhi and kept another bunch for himself.

"What's the prize?" Beck and Bodhi asked at the same time.

"Pride, not prize. Half the proceeds from the carnival today go to the children's hospital." Bowen picked up a basketball and, still facing them, shot it backward over his shoulder, and even though the rim was angled to make it nearly impossible to drain a shot, the ball swooshed through the net.

"In or out?" Bowen challenged, his grayish-blue eyes narrowed even as his dark brows arched in a look that was so familiar Beck's heart rate kicked up and his spirit soared. His oldest cousin had often laid down challenges for him and Bodhi. And the familiarity—being together, egging each other on—felt so right, when the past couple of months had felt so off for him.

Of course it was game on—basketball shots, darts at balloons, Skee-Ball. Between the three of them, they amassed quite a collection of colorful, fuzzy creatures that they handed out to young children arriving with their parents to try their luck before the rodeo finals.

They also drew more than their share of female attention—something Bodhi often took advantage of. But Beck, who'd had the same girl since high school who now worked on the pro rodeo staff even after receiving her MS in public health four years ago, had never once considered taking advantage of what Ashni had declared to be "one of his many superpowers—being way too easy on the eyes."

He'd never even kissed another girl and had only once speculated about it a couple of months ago with his cousins in a bar one night after he'd bombed in the finals that evening and had been feeling particularly out of sorts.

He'd be lying if he hadn't thought about it a few more times since, especially as he and Ash seemed out of sync. It was messing with his head and his performance. His wins and money were down, and the joy was gone. Riding and roping and bulldogging felt like a job he had to slog through instead of an adventure.

Ash always brought the light and magic, and lately he'd felt alone. Her taking two weeks for her cousin's wedding couldn't have come at a worse time for him, and he knew absolutely he was being unfair. He understood family and commitments. But he missed her and felt unsettled without her and watching Bodhi chat and flirt with various women including a busty blonde whom he handed a large blue bear to and autographed the bear's white tummy, felt somehow dangerous. Beck had been privy to Bodhi's sexy charm offensive since high school—watching him flirt women out of their panties and most everything else as effortlessly as he'd order a beer at a honky-tonk.

He knew he didn't want that. Even as he wondered what it would be like to let the flirt unspool just a little, the idea made him feel dirty.

He had to get his head on straight before his events. Beck handed off his last fuzzy win to a child when a prize at another booth caught his eye.

"You don't see that every day." Bodhi laughed at the large plush horse rearing up, a paintbrush in its mouth and a rainbow of colors on a palette sewn onto one hoof. A red beret perched jauntily on its head.

"I want to win it for Ashni," Beck declared. Ash had studied studio art along with epidemiology in college. When he and his cousins retired from the tour and moved to their granddad's Montana ranch, he'd build her an art studio.

"It's huge," Bowen said, Mister Practical. "It will take up

the back seat of your truck."

"I'm going to win it."

If he won the quirky-looking artist horse, maybe he wouldn't feel so guilty. And Ashni would know that even when she was back home in Denver participating in her cousin's elaborate three-day wedding, he'd been thinking of her. She'd also know that he still thought of her as the artist—the singer, studio artist, and science nerd—he'd first fallen in love with.

She was due back this afternoon. Maybe instead of heading straight to the ranch, they'd have a quiet dinner—just them. And a hotel. His blood and hope surged.

"Bet she kicks you out of bed in favor of the plush." Bodhi grinned. "Let's do it. I'll help."

Bodhi strode up to the booth. Ping-pong balls had to be tossed into small glass bowls with narrow lips and a goldfish swimming inside.

"I don't need help." Beck strode after him.

"You both need your heads examined." Bowen followed them. "You're going to end up with an aquarium of goldfish—not exactly conducive to a life on the road. Buy her a damn ring already. Be practical. You need the space."

"Yeah. That's why he should ball and chain it—a ring will save space in his truck." Bodhi snorted.

Beck's chest seized.

A ring. A diamond. Forever. He wanted forever with Ash. But not yet. He wasn't ready. He still had a lot to prove. Money to earn. And he wasn't leaving his cousins on the tour without him. They'd always had each other's backs. Always. And then there was his mother's marriage examples he couldn't quite shake off.

"Plenty of time for a ring," Beck said with more ease than he felt. "When we retire. All of us." He looked at his cousins to ensure that they knew he was keeping the promise they'd made so long ago. Then he handed over the rest of his tickets and stepped to the line.

It took Bodhi's help to win the grand prize, and he'd no more than headed out of the games area flanked by his cousins so he could go prepare for his three events in the finals—steer wrestling, calf roping and saddle bronc riding—when he saw a young girl clutching a box of crayons and the pro rodeo tour coloring book staring at him, her mouth wide open.

"You're the cowboy on the cover." She held up the book for him to see. The coloring books were free to kids. Ashni had amused herself sketching many of the cowboys last year on the tour, and she'd turned her line drawings into a coloring book. The tour paid the printing fees and gave out the books to kids at every rodeo event. Ashni had been so excited in her own quiet way. She'd shyly admitted that it had made her feel like she was still an artist, and it was a way to give back to the community.

"I am." He smiled at the young girl, who looked to be maybe seven or eight. She was pale and frail. He saw a port peeking out of her loose-fitting pink T-shirt with a bucking horse in rhinestones that hung off her thin shoulders.

His heart broke a little each time he saw a kid battling a life-threatening disease, but he still went to the pediatric wards at a hospital in most of the cities he hit on the tour, Ashni by his side. She would draw with kids or sit and play her guitar and sing.

"I'm going to be an artist when I grow up," she said. "It just takes practice, wanting it and expiration." Her voice was thin, but her eyes glowed with determination. Her hair was wispy blonde on her head, just growing back.

"Inspiration," her mother whispered, smiling at her daughter, her hand smoothing over her daughter's narrow shoulders.

No man by her side and no ring, Beck noted, feeling more despair sweep through him. How could a man ever leave his child and the mother of his child, especially during an illness?

But men left. He knew it first-hand. His cousins knew it too.

"Well then—" he squatted down "—maybe this guy can help inspire you." He handed her the artistic horse.

The girl's eyes got huge. "Really? For me?" she whispered. The horse was nearly as large as she was.

Her mother blinked hard. "Are you sure?"

"Yes, ma'am."

"Bless you," she whispered.

He stood. "My pleasure, ma'am." He handed her two tickets that would get her in the VIP section for the finals.

"It's too much," she breathed. "The tour already gave the

hospital tickets for many families."

"Seats are more comfortable in this section, and the food and drink vendors come to you. Enjoy your day."

"What's the horse's name?" the little girl asked, tugging on his hand while her other arm wrapped tightly around the animal.

He had no idea. It was her choice, wasn't it?

"Absolution," Bodhi answered. "The horse's name is Absolution."

What the heck? Beck opened his mouth to tell the girl his cousin was teasing, but she gazed at the plush animal's comical expression with a steadfast devotion that broke his heart a little more.

"Hello, Abso…abso something. I'm Amanda."

"Pleased to meet you, Amanda." He touched her head softly and tipped his hat. "Ma'am."

He and his cousins walked back to the arena.

"Smart move," Bowen said. "You did a good deed and don't have storage issues."

"But you're also out a mea culpa gift for Ashni," Bodhi added. "Might I suggest a big, sparkly ring that will blind other drooling cowboys from across the bar and howl in a true Neanderthal style 'this one's taken, boys.'"

Beck increased his speed.

"Get her a ring or cut her loose. This is embarrassing," Bodhi called out.

Beck peeled off to the dressing room so he could put on his chaps and wrap his ribs. He pulled off his tee, grabbed one of the many rolls of tape and began to wrap. When he competed, he wore a Kevlar vest, but the tape offered protection and stability for his often aching ribs.

"You're in trouble, cuz. I can feel it." Of course Bodhi couldn't leave him alone.

Beck shoved in his mouth guard so he didn't say something he'd later regret.

"If you love her…" Bodhi picked up the medical tape to wrap Beck's shoulder even though he'd been pretty injury-free even this late in the season "…I don't see why you're cowering outside of the chute."

Lovely image. Beck pulled out his mouth guard. "I don't need relationship advice from a man whose relationships last an hour."

Bodhi expertly finished the wrap and ripped off the tape with his teeth.

"I last way longer than that," he taunted, flipping his wrist so the mouth guard jammed back in Beck's mouth. "Maybe that's the problem."

Beck yanked out his mouth guard again.

But Bodhi beat him to the punch line. "You should have kept the horse. Least you'd have some company in bed." Bodhi tipped his hat and was gone, leaving Beck to flip off empty space.

ASHNI FINISHED PACKING as slow as she dared. The entire

wedding party and many guests were meeting for a late brunch in the hotel, and then she was heading to the airport—much to her parents' disappointment.

Usually she was happy to get back to Beck, but she was still smarting from the pointed questions about her lack of marital status and reminders of her age from supposedly loving and well-meaning family and friends.

Usually she blew it off. But even her parents had sat her down this time and demanded to know her plans and what she was doing with her life.

Hurtful. It's not like she didn't have accomplishments. She was making a difference to a lot of kids who were rodeo fans, but now, she was having doubts. It had started at Christmas. She'd been thinking this was the year Beck would propose. But he hadn't. Instead, he'd signed up for another year on the tour before discussing it with her. She'd been stunned. She wanted to stop living a life on the road, but she hadn't told him. She'd been upset there was no ring. And that hurt and pissed her off because she shouldn't rely on Beck for her happiness.

Her passivity irked her.

She glared at her reflection in the mirror. "You are your own woman. Educated. Talented. A professional. You don't need a proposal to complete you. You're just twenty-nine not forty."

She needed her usual calm but instead felt anxious. And her stomach swirled nauseatingly, something it had been doing more often lately. Too busy with work and planning the art classes she'd teach over a week break in Montana, she'd barely had time to breathe, much less eat a meal.

"Marriage isn't everything." She faced her reflection, hands on hips, willing the information to sink fully into her psyche. Really, she was letting her mom's doubts and her aunties' clamoring ruin what should have been a precious and beautiful memory with Reeva and her family.

"Get over it," she muttered zipping her suitcase shut. Her Indian clothes were already in a garment bag ready for her parents to take home.

"Be the woman you want to be," she reminded herself in the elevator down.

She was in charge of her own happiness. Feeling bolstered by her pep talk, she went downstairs to the lobby and immediately wished she'd stayed in her room. Her mother fretted she was pale and thin. Her father was still angry that Beck hadn't taken the weekend off to attend the wedding. He harangued her and anyone who would listen about what kind of boy was he, playing games instead of getting a real job.

And then he sat her down and called over Anju, the wife of his oldest friend and a successful matchmaker, who began interviewing her about what kind of boy she wanted. Yes, her father, who had immigrated to the United States in middle school, was suddenly intent on arranging a marriage for her.

What kind of a boy did she want?

Not even Beck at this point.

Ash contemplated becoming celibate. She too was upset

he hadn't come to the wedding—not the full two weeks, but he could have come for the weekend, missing only one rodeo. Ashni showing up solo had NOT gone unnoticed by anyone.

She was so relieved when Reeva and John appeared that she launched herself off the chair and practically tackled her cousin.

"Do you want to hide in one of my suitcases and I'll spring you at the airport?" Reeva laughed.

"Yes, please." Ashni was a bit embarrassed at how desperate she sounded. "Now that you're hitched, all the marriage juju is going to be hurled at me like monkey poop."

John laughed. "It's not that bad."

"It's worse," she and Reeva answered at the same time, and then Reeva hugged her.

"It's fine. You have Beck. Don't let any of the family pressure you."

Self-actualized words she reminded herself of over and over during brunch as her father continued to push his dump Beck theme. It was weird. Her father was pretty hip and happily immersed in both Indian and American cultures. He'd fallen in love with a beautiful strawberry blonde from San Francisco in med school and had defied his parents and married her in Vegas one weekend before their separate residencies started. But now he was talking arranged marriage, having her finally apply to medical school, and packing her up back to Denver.

She was more than a decade beyond his ability to boss

her, but still, it hurt that they didn't approve of her life. She was a pleaser by nature, and all the side-eyes had left their mark, and she felt bruised. Reeva had always been the one to casually flaunt public opinion, and no matter who said what, she kept her good nature.

Not Ash. She was sure there was some meditation she should be chanting about peace and calm and understanding as she pushed food around on her plate.

She didn't need to head to the airport for another hour, but maybe she should escape now. She was flying into Boise so she and Beck could drive to his granddad's ranch in Montana. Beck would help his granddad on the family's legacy ranch and compete at the Copper Mountain Rodeo, and she would teach an art class at an after-school program called Harry's House.

She'd never taught before but Sky Wilder, who was an accomplished metals artist and married to one of the top bull riders in the world before he retired this year, had contacted her after seeing the coloring book and rodeo comic story she'd included in the back.

It would be good to feel like an artist again. And she loved working with kids.

She checked her watch and then scrolled through her phone, hoping to catch Beck's first event—bulldogging. She loved watching him. He was so fast and fluid and fearless. And sexy. Her tummy flipped just thinking about him, and her anger and frustration faded a little.

"Oh, hey." Reeva waved imperiously to get the bartender's attention. "You have satellite, right? Find the rodeo channel. Please." She smiled the last word.

Not many people ever said no to Reeva, and soon forty people were watching Beck on Raider fly over the line while Bodhi kept the galloping steer straight and practically before she blinked, Beck had slid off Raider, grabbed the horns, and with a quick twist, the bull was on its back legs up and then Beck released, popped to his feet and waved to the crowd with his hat.

"What?" John turned to her. "What just happened?"

"Fierce athleticism and magic." Ashni felt her heart swell with pride.

Beck's time was faster than any of the other cowboys by more than two seconds. And then he was being awarded his buckle and prize money.

"Ladies and gentlemen," the announcer Jerry Williams's voice rang out over the PA system with its familiar, warm timbre. "Please give a round of applause to your Idaho Panhandle Pro Rodeo steer wrestling champion this weekend: Beckett Ballantyne."

Beck strode into the arena still wearing his electric-blue chaps with white stars and tipped his hat to the crowd. Ashni felt her heart leap. This never got old even though she'd seen Beck in the winner's circle many times.

And then everything went pear-shaped. Usually the awards were fast—one question from Jerry, a couple of sentences and thanks to the crowd and then pictures with the sponsors, but this time Jerry was spinning it out—throwing out hints and asking questions about the Copper Mountain Rodeo and going home with his "special lady."

Weird.

Ashni frowned. What was Jerry doing? But as he continued to push Beck—asking him if he had any special plans with his lady over his short break—it became unfortunately clear what game Jerry was playing.

Ashni felt sick to her stomach, but she laughed, twisted her hair into a low bun at the back on her neck and tried to stomp down the unusual combination of anger, humiliation and tears as Beck dodged the questions, looking as awkward as a snowboarder would at a pool. Beck said he didn't have anything special planned. Ashni avoided looking at the anger stamped on her father's face and the pity filling her mom's gaze.

She quickly made the rounds, hugging everyone, saying she'd see them all at Christmas if not before and then she made her escape into the Denver sun, wheeling her suitcase toward her ride share even as she made changes to her flight.

✪

MORE THAN AN hour after Jerry pulled his stunt putting Beck in the hot seat, Beck still felt riled. He'd come in third in the saddle bronc after he'd started in first. The prize money and buckle should have been his.

He knew his success hinged on preparation and focus. Why had he let Jerry get to him? Bodhi had probably put

Jerry up to the stunt—totally juvenile, but he hadn't needed to respond in kind. He felt disloyal, as if he'd publicly rejected Ash, insinuating she wasn't special. Instead he'd been rejecting the spectacle and publicity. He hated being put on the spot.

He needed to stop worrying. He and Ash were solid. But thank God she'd been at the wedding, likely too busy to watch.

She hadn't texted him like she usually did before and after he competed when she wasn't present, nor had she checked in last night or answered his text.

Probably busy.

She and Reeva were as tight as he was with his cousins. He checked his watch. He had time before her flight arrived.

He headed back to the ridiculous ping-pong and fishbowl game, hoping to win the other massive artistic horse grand prize the guy had put up after he'd won the first, only this time he didn't have Bodhi's help and his hold hand was aching something fierce. Usually he iced it after a ride, and Ashni would gently massage his hand, stretch the muscles and tendons.

"Deal, cowboy," he scolded. Ash had better things to do than coddle him. Still, he couldn't shake the weird feeling he had in his belly. Winning the second grand prize for Ashni, even though it was wildly impractical, would make him feel better. Except it wasn't there.

"'Nuther cowboy won it over an hour ago. Didn't miss a shot. Never seen nothing like it," the attendant explained.

"Still plenty of other things to win to charm your lady or lots of ladies." He laughed.

But not the horse.

And Beck had no idea why winning the ridiculous-looking artistic horse seemed so imperative. It was weird. Bulky. Impractical. They lived their lives on the road—motel rooms or the small living suite in his rig.

He walked back toward the livestock stalls, muttering some not nice terms about uber-skilled ping-pong-chucking cowboys under his breath.

He'd buy her something special in Marietta. Take her somewhere nice to dinner tonight, although he cringed thinking about all the wedding talk. Between Bodhi and Jerry, he was starting to feel like he had a target on his chest.

He entered the area where the competition horses were held. The dimmer light and familiar smell of the animals and sawdust instantly soothed him in a way that people—except Ash—never could.

He came to Raider's stall and the champion quarter horse shook out his flowing black mane and snorted a welcome. The last of Beck's tension drained from his body. He greeted Raider, scratching his majestic neck and silky mane. He complimented the horse on how well he'd done and snuck him a few treats as they walked to the horse trailer.

Raider tossed his head and whinnied as if basking in the compliments. He walked like a champion. He'd definitely been on his game today in his two final events.

Beck walked him to his rig and up the ramp firmly. Raider never liked this part. He no longer balked, but every gleaming muscle tensed.

Beck spoke softly to him and secured him in the trailer using his voice and body to reassure and praise. He smoothed his callused hand down Raider's gleaming and muscled shoulder and finger-combed his silky black mane.

"Done good today," he said softly. He took his two new buckles—a first in steer wrestling and another in tie-down roping—and held them out for Raider to sniff. It was a ritual for them both. And over the past six years he'd been on the pro rodeo circuit, quite often he and Raider had come out on top.

Raider snorted and nuzzled his shirt pocket, looking for the expected treat.

"Greedy," he teased. "I already gave you two apple slices." He laughed softly and scratched Raider's forelock before slipping him a carrot and another slice of apple.

Raider's velvety nostrils and mouth tickled his palm, and Beckett smiled, gave the horse another pat, and then checked his water and feed for the trip home to Marietta before adding another layer of bedding for the trailer.

"Behave now," he cautioned. "And I'll go get your partner in crime." He walked down the short ramp. "After that we need to head to the airport so I can find mine."

He re-entered the arena stables and headed straight to Gallatin, who seemed judgy, as if offended at being passed over for Raider.

"I've got you," he soothed, amused by the spirited horse. He'd already decided not to sell him.

His phone rang. His heart soared.

"Hey, baby, your flight early?"

"Hey, baby? Is that how you greet your mother?"

Beck winced. His mom, Madelyn Leigh Ballantyne, had never gone by Maddy nor had she deigned to dump her maiden name upon marrying any of her four husbands—all soon discarded. None of her sisters had either, as if the Ballantyne name signaled royalty.

It didn't, although in Marietta and the large surrounding ranching community, the name meant something special. But all three daughters had fled the ranch for college and a life far more urban than Montana's wild beauty and wide-open spaces. By the time he and his cousins had been competing in high school rodeo, their mothers had all been divorced and their dads all out of the picture, so the three of them had started competing using their mothers' maiden name.

"Sorry, I was expecting Ash."

Her sigh was epic. "Genevieve said that Bodhi scored higher than you in the saddle bronc."

Ouch.

He refrained from defending himself by reminding her of his two wins today. No doubt her sisters had already informed her of those as well. His mom and two aunts had been harassing them for years to quit the rodeo, grow up, get real jobs, and become men, but they tracked their points and earnings and wins more obsessively than their offspring.

"It's so like him to enter late in another event that is your specialty just to show off."

Beck had learned a long time ago to keep his mouth mostly shut.

"I wanted to let you know I will see you at the ranch Tuesday."

"You'll what?" He stumbled against the temporary corral fencing. Gallatin stomped his left front hoof, and Beck barely dodged it.

"You could at least pretend to be pleased." His mother's cultured tones hardened slightly. "Last I checked, I am still your mother, and you are my only child, Beckett Alexander Morgan Ballantyne."

Not for the first time did he think his mom should have had more children. Even though she was the CEO of the largest commercial property management company in Denver and was on several charitable boards, she still had too much time to scrutinize his every move.

"But you hate Montana."

"If you think I'm going to let my sisters woo Daddy to gain more of their share of inheritance, you're wrong—as you often are."

"Granddad is still alive." His teeth clenched. "Spoke to him this morning."

"You didn't speak to me this morning."

True.

Bodhi would have had her laughing. Bowen would never

have pissed her off. He felt like his mom barely tolerated him and had lost all patience with him before he entered high school.

"I wasn't planning to show up on your doorstep for two weeks."

Wrong thing to say. Of course.

"You should. You are always visiting your granddad, not your mother. And…"

Beck knew exactly what she was going to say next.

"It's long beyond time you gave up that childish lifestyle and settled down with Ash, if she's your choice, and get a real job and start a family. You are running down the clock."

"I just turned twenty-eight. I'm hardly an AARP member."

"Well, your grandfather is well beyond AARP," she shot back.

"He's not even eighty yet."

"Eighty is ancient. He should be in a condo. Relaxing."

Beck couldn't even begin to picture that—the condo or his granddad relaxing.

"Your granddad is getting too old to run that ranch. It's ridiculous for…" He must have hit the mute with his cheek as he finished with Gallatin and led the horse to his rig. The silence didn't matter. His mom and aunts regularly railed on about how their father should sell the ranch to a developer or rich celebrity or tech giant and move to Denver so they could watch over him.

His granddad wouldn't last ten minutes with their fussing and skyscrapers blocking his views.

He rolled his eyes and unmuted the phone. His mom was still talking. He arrived at his trailer.

"Granddad will never sell," he said firmly. "The ranch has been in the Ballantyne family since long before the railroad arrived in Marietta."

"Stop drinking that Kool-Aid," his mom sniped. "He's too old to be living there alone."

"He's not alone. He has ranch hands, and one or all of us are there every break in the tour."

"He's barely hanging on," his mom accused. "Holding out hope that one of you boys will ever think of anyone other than yourselves and settle down on the ranch. Not that I want you to do that," she hastily tagged on.

Beck opened his mouth, but his mom continued. "You boys need to stop wasting your lives on the rodeo. One of you is going to get hurt and then where will you be? You have an economics degree and a minor in statistics. You'll totally waste an excellent education if you're out there riding the range, becoming a broke, broken-down cowboy. It's absurd, like some spaghetti western movie. It's time to change the channel."

Usually he and Ashni laughed over his mom and aunts' pot shots at their careers. She said her aunties were worse. Beck wasn't sure about that.

"He needs to sell so none of you waste your lives on his silly dreams. Legacy," she huffed. "And if he won't sell it, we will."

Beck stumbled on the ramp leading into the trailer. Gallatin took advantage and balked, but Beck quickly regained control.

His mom had never sounded this adamant before, and dread trickled through him. His granddad was healthy, wasn't he? Beck mentally replayed the conversation from this morning and nearly missed his mom's grand conclusion.

"Anyway, don't worry," she said breezily, which made his stomach cramp. "We have everything planned. We'll see you all on Tuesday. We've got a crew coming to spruce up the outside of the house and do some upgrades inside. We've also got a list for you boys to knock off for the barn and cabin up on Plum Hill. Dumb name, but the view is decent. We're going to help Daddy throw the biggest and last Ballantyne Bash, and then we'll get the ranch on the market."

"You can't railroad Granddad," Beck said even though his mom had one setting: wrecking-ball efficiency. Her way or jump out of her way.

"Sweetie, it's for the best. Trust me."

He didn't. "Text me your flight details. One of us will pick you up." That was definitely going to require several best out of rock, paper, scissors rounds as neither he, Bowen, nor Bodhi would volunteer for that trip.

"We've rented a car. And we have one of those POD things being delivered. This will be for the best for everyone."

His mom hung up, and Beck stared out of his trailer at

the parking lot, which was beginning to clear out as cowboys headed home or to the next rodeo.

Packing up five generations of Ballantyne life was going to take a heck of a lot more than a PODS container. And Beck wasn't going to let his granddad be pushed in or out of anything without a fight.

Chapter Two

Ashni had enough time to think in the airport. She bought a Starbucks chai and walked the terminal, earbuds in, listening to the soundtrack of *Hamilton*, which always motivated her. Maybe she was overreacting. She definitely felt overwrought. Why did she want to marry Beck anyway? That burned. She was young, educated, talented, earned good money, had options. She had a master's in public health as well as a BS in epidemiology and a BA in studio arts. And yet, here she was, waiting, hoping.

Why should she be eager to marry at twenty-nine?

Her elaborate *mehndi*—the henna tattoo that covered her palms, the backs of her hands and scrolled up her arms—taunted her. She'd always imagined having a big Indian wedding—so many family and friends celebrating her. And they'd add in whatever traditions Beck wanted.

But it was a show—which was probably what appealed to her love of drama and the spectacularly vivid visuals. Beck was private, a bit shy. He'd hate that. He'd do it with a smile on his face, backed by his cousins—Bowen stoic and helpful; Bodhi flip but scrutinizing her with an intensity she'd never understood. And Indian weddings were lavishly expensive.

Beck saved as much money as he could to invest in the ranch. Another goal they'd never talked about. It was just a given. And she'd gone along with it because she loved Beck, and she'd come to love his cousins, granddad and Montana. She liked the smaller towns over cities.

She stopped walking, chai halfway to her lips.

What was her deal? Was she passive? No goals of her own?

Doubt washed over her. Shame.

Since earning her master's, she'd just started following Beck's lead. The tour had sounded fun for a year or two—seeing the country. She'd started working in marketing and had really enjoyed it at first. She'd done community outreach and had focused her efforts on children's hospitals and organizations that supported families in communities where the tour went, and Ashni was proud of the network she'd established.

She wasn't a buckle bunny looking for a free ride and some fun.

But this year it had all soured.

She'd always figured they would build their lives and she her career once he retired from the tour, but it had been five years now. Traveling was becoming a grind. She wanted a home. A garden. A full kitchen to cook meals. A baby. And when she'd asked about marriage right after Christmas, he'd changed the subject.

And then she'd heard him speculating with Bodhi about being with so many different women—did it feel different when he…? Ashni cut off that train of thought. It still hurt when she thought about it.

Was Beck bored?

He didn't seem bored. He was just as affectionate, tender, always looking for fun things to do on the road. So what changed?

Me.

I'm bored.

Not with Beck. But with the lifestyle. And she was taking it out on him. She slowly sat down in an available blue chair nowhere near her gate. They wanted different things. He was young and healthy. He could compete for years still unless he got seriously injured. He was younger than his cousins who showed no sign of slowing down. Bowen was nearly three years older. Did she want to be doing this for three more years?

Hell no.

So that was her answer wasn't it? She noted her hand holding the chai shook, and her detachment spooked her. Time to get a grip. She took a bracing swallow of the sweet, still-hot liquid and closed her eyes, focusing on the silky texture, the taste and heat as she swallowed. She needed to make the changes she wanted and find her own happiness. Stop relying on Beck.

She didn't want to be one of those women who followed a man blindly, putting him first and never herself and taking out her bitterness on Beck because she'd been too weak to act on her own behalf.

"Okay, no more Miss Passive," she coached. "Time to start building a life you want."

Ashni finished her chai, and after a moment of hesitation, got up and bought another. She'd been feeling wonky lately. Not hungry. Nothing sounded appetizing, and yet the chai felt wonderful heating her tummy. Maybe now that the wedding was over and she'd had her bolstering heart-to-heart with herself, her appetite would return.

She took her second chai and walked to her gate, visualizing a game plan. This week would help because she'd be doing something new: teaching the art class. And she'd be in her favorite town in all of America, the town she always thought she and Beck would settle in and raise their children.

She'd have the week to get some things in motion, but she'd need some space from Beck to do so because it would be so easy to fall back into bed and their routine if she didn't. Ashni did not want to have the same conversation with herself this time next year.

Finals were at the end of next month, and then Beck would have a break to make some choices of his own.

Pick us. Choose me.

Panic swirled through her, and she wished she could call Reeva to talk about everything, but Reeva would be heading off on her honeymoon soon. Ash didn't want to bother her with her airport anguish.

Since changing her flight, Ashni had another half hour before boarding. She texted Sky Wilder to ask if her cousin-in-law's Marietta studio apartment on Bramble Lane was still available for the week. Sky had offered it for free since the class didn't pay, but Ashni had demurred knowing that Beck would want to stay at the ranch.

But now it's about what I want.

She also texted that she would be flying into Bozeman, not traveling with Beck. Sky said the apartment was open and offered to pick her up so they could chat on the way into town. Ashni happily accepted. She didn't need a car in Marietta. Everything was so walkable. Even as she wondered how Beck would take her change in plans, she crushed the thought. She had to think about herself and what she wanted now.

She booted up her computer and resolutely crafted a resignation letter to her boss. This was it. The beginning of a new life. She hit send.

There should have been a lighting change. Softer music in a different key, the sound slowly swelling. The chorus softly singing and then the strings working up to her solo, and she'd stand, spotlit and... Laughing at herself, she googled some job boards in public health first in Denver but then in Montana—she could hope that she and Beck could find their way, and she'd grown to love Marietta and the Three Tree Ranch as much as he and his cousins did. And his granddad felt like her granddad.

Her stomach dropped. By staying in town, she'd also miss time with Ben. She called him. Told him that she wouldn't be staying at the ranch because of the class.

"What's Beck done to be in the doghouse?" His deep voice rumbled.

"Nothing, it's just more convenient," she said hastily.

"Talked to him this morning, and he said you and he would be driving in this evening."

Darn.

"Ummmmm…"

The laugh that rolled out warmed her heart. "Good for you. 'Bout time. Stay strong. No doubt Beck needs the kick in his ass."

"It's not a you-know-what kicking," she reiterated. "I just…"

"It's an ass-kicking. He needs it. Bodhi needs one too." He paused. "Well, that would be something."

Ashni scrunched her face, not understanding.

"You stay strong. Don't give in when he comes round your door all full of apologies. Make him work for it."

He was making her sound manipulative. Was she? "I really just—" She blew out a breath. "I really need to figure things out, and Beck gets around me so easily. I don't think straight. So, some space."

Ben laughed again. "It's a Ballantyne trait. We make women lose their good sense. Don't talk to him. Make him crazy. Spin it out 'til the end of the week."

That made it sound like a game.

"Shouldn't you be on his side if there were sides?" she demanded.

"I am," he said. "But I'm on yours too. You do your part.

Don't cave. I'll do mine."

He hung up. Typical of Ben. He never said goodbye. He'd stand in the front, tall, fit, strong as Copper Mountain, give a quick wave or a grunt and walk to the barn, his back the only witness to his grandsons driving away.

Ashni clutched her phone. She needed to text Beck and tell him she wouldn't be at the Boise airport. She didn't want to tell him until his events were over. She checked the time. She'd text him after boarding. Something dinged on her search parameters, and she stared at the new posting. It was too surreal. Too perfect.

Feeling a spurt of reckless sprinkled with giddy, Ashni uploaded her résumé and wrote a short statement of intent. She nibbled on her lip as she read over her letter and then hit send.

"Grass growing under my feet no longer."

And as she took her seat that she'd upgraded, she said yes to a glass of prosecco. Texted Beck her change of plans and promptly switched her phone to airplane mode.

"Cheers," she said to the businesswoman next to her.

BECK DROVE HIS rig—his cousins not far behind—past the oh-so-familiar large, white, two-story farmhouse and continued on to the looming red barn, framed by sturdy oaks, a few hundred yards away. He parked to make it easy to unload his horses and unhitch his rig. His cousins followed suit.

The breeze, so familiar and scented with pine, blew down from the Gallatin Mountain range that towered over the north border of the ranch nestled into the foothills. The ranch was his favorite place in the country—and he'd traveled a lot. It was where he felt most himself. And the rolling foothills, covered in richest pasture grass—some of which they sold—pines and native fauna were the most beautiful sights in the world to him, when he'd head down Highway 89 and see the ranch and Paradise Valley spread out below him, welcoming him.

This was paradise. Home. And it always centered him, but not tonight.

Because Ashni wasn't here.

"Did you get a phone call from hell?" Bodhi demanded.

"No, a text."

"Maddy texted?" Bodhi asked incredulously.

No one called Madelyn *Maddy* ever. Nor did anyone but Bodhi call his mom—Genevieve Suzanne—Jenny, Viv or Suze. Not even her father. And Bodhi wouldn't say any of those nicknames to her face.

"What? No." He shook his head. He'd had hours to brood over Ashni's text that she was staying in town because it was more convenient. How the hell was staying nearly a twenty-minute drive away from him convenient?

And what would she do in town? He'd be busy on the ranch with chores and upgrades. She often helped when they were home and cooked up meals like a chef competing on a network foody show. She loved playing in the kitchen and left Granddad a freezer full of food. A couple of years ago he and his cousins had upgraded the kitchen for her. Beck had built new butcher block countertops and cabinets and open shelves, and they'd all pitched in on new and upgraded appliances.

But he always made time to go into town with her or let her borrow his truck. How many men would be okay with that? Beck had tried to call her multiple times today, possibly veering into stalker mode, but she hadn't picked up. Not once.

He couldn't make sense of it. They hadn't had a fight. They never fought. Not like he'd seen lots of couples do on the road. The rodeo folks were a passionate crowd, but Beck and Ashni had always saved their passion for the bedroom. Two weeks since he'd seen her. Held her. Made love to her, and now she wasn't here. What kind of BS was that? His stomach cramped and his head pounded.

Maybe he was sick.

Not heartbroke.

"Earth to Beck." Bodhi waved a hand in front of his face. He slapped it away.

"Yeah, Mom called." He tried to get his head back into the conversation. Bodhi eyed him suspiciously. Maybe he should become a cop after the rodeo. That would actually be a funny TV show. He'd charm confessions out of all his suspects. "She's coming. They're all coming," he said gloomily.

"Did she mention sprucing up the house to put the

ranch on the market?" Bowen asked just as their granddad appeared on the porch.

They all waved.

"Yeah."

"So what was the text from hell?" Bodhi never let anything go, but Beck wasn't sharing his trouble. If there was trouble. And definitely not to Bodhi, who had predicted problems today.

Never give a man ammunition to shoot when you've already shot yourself in the foot.

But what had he done?

Sure, it had been hella awkward with Jerry for a few moments today in the winner's circle, but Ash had been far away. Yes, he should have attended the wedding. But he couldn't afford missing any events. He'd dropped in points this year, but Bodhi and Bowen were on fire.

"Must be bad if you're ignoring me." Bodhi followed him as he unlocked his trailer doors.

"I'm not. Just got work to do and want to see Granddad."

"And I'm supposed to just ignore the fact that Ash isn't with you?"

"Yup." He hopped in his trailer.

Bodhi stared up at him speculatively and then began humming under his breath, something he should obviously recognize since Bodhi smirked.

"Going to…"

"Leave it until Grey's tonight." Bowen slapped his work

gloves against Bodhi's face, interrupting the song as Granddad approached.

"Yes, Dad." Bodhi grinned and then turned to Granddad for a full-on embrace—no one-armed side hug and back or shoulder slap for Bodhi.

Maybe that's why women loved him.

Everyone did.

Loved and admired and indulged.

The social part, the celebrity part, had always been harder for Beck. He tried to emulate Bodhi. Fell short. But got back up and tried again. Ash always made social situations easy. She was so quick to smile and engage and encourage everyone. She oozed peace and concern. Entering that high school music room after seeing the most beautiful girl in the world through the window singing was still hands down the smartest thing he'd ever done.

He'd seen her and known she was the one. Part of his future. Half his life now. And nothing that had happened in the intervening years had sown one seed of doubt.

So why was he so unsettled? And why was something that had always been so easy suddenly so hard?

While they took care of their horses and put them in stalls, they chatted with Granddad about the ranch, the rodeo, the usual things. It was all so normal—no mention of the moms' visit or possibly selling—but Beck felt darn near to crawling out of his skin with stress. He'd texted Ashni, wanting to meet up tonight—just them—a sacrilege since Sunday night was always dinner at the ranch, Ashni cooking

Granddad's favorite, chicken tikka masala, and then a beer at Grey's with a round of pool. Maybe a bit of dancing and then home.

He'd asked if he could pick her up so they could take a drive or go out to dinner. No answer.

"Something smells good." Bowen sniffed appreciatively as they all stepped into the mudroom and toed off their boots, lining them up like they always did.

"Your favorite, Granddad," Beck burst out, recognizing the savory scent, and the relief that poured through him weakened his knees so that he stumbled over a splinter in the floor.

He hopped and pulled it out. Refinishing the floors was on the to-do list this week or next, although with the moms here that might be impossible. He tried to stroll into the kitchen slightly less eager than he'd been, but he needn't have bothered. Ash wasn't here.

"Where's Ash?" he asked looking around.

"She and that cute little gal married to Kane Wilder and a couple of her sisters-in-law came over a few hours ago with bags of groceries. Ashni gave a master class in cooking her chicken tikka masala, veggie biryani, chana, and then Bodhi's favorite saag. Oh, and they made a stack of chapatis as long as my arm. All the gals were rolling them out, messing them up and laughing and talking a mile every minute."

Granddad lifted the lid on one pot, and the fragrance was mouthwatering.

"I sat right there and watched it all. Drank a beer, ate a

couple of chapatis as their official taste tester. Had a good time. The house was alive."

He looked at Beck. "Even though she's busy this week, she didn't want me to miss out on my favorite meal. Sweet girl. Keeper."

Of course he was keeping her. "Busy?"

"How could you forget between winning and giving away the art horse and now?" Bodhi demanded.

"Huh?"

"She's teaching an art class this week at Harry's House," both Granddad and Bodhi said at the same time.

"Storytelling through art," Bowen added. "The kids have one wall in the teen room to create a mural."

Awareness shot through Beck and he all but slapped his forehead. He knew that. She'd been working on plans for it for over a month now. She'd been so excited that he'd felt guilty that she hadn't had the chance to teach before. And then the awkwardness between them, and the missed wedding, Jerry, a crap ride, his mom's visit and bombshell.

"Slipped my mind," he muttered when all three of them stared at him like he was slightly deranged. "Momentarily."

So that was why he'd wanted the plush. To celebrate her opportunity and accomplishment. His subconscious had been trying to nudge the rest of him to wake up and pay attention.

"Let's eat," Bowen said.

"Then you can try to climb out of the doghouse," Bodhi added.

"She seemed real happy," Granddad said, oblivious to his tension. "She had this tattoo thing all over her hands. Not permanent, but it will last a few weeks. Said it was from the wedding party. Looked real pretty."

"Mehndi," Beck said, feeling hollow.

"That was it," Granddad said. "Showed me some pictures. Real fancy getups the girls wear. So much gold they glitter like Christmas trees. Men too. Colors so bright they hurt your eyes. Beer?"

They washed their hands. Beck got the beer. Bowen set the table and Bodhi poured the water. It was all so familiar—the kitchen, the routine, the meal, and yet utterly foreign because Ash wasn't here.

And all the light and warmth had been sucked from the room because she was gone. They dished up straight from the stove and sat down at the farmhouse table that had been built by Granddad's daddy.

Beck sat down next to his grandfather. His chicken and biryani cooled while the conversation swirled around him, Bodhi holding court, Granddad catching them up on the ranch and the news of Marietta. He had no idea how his granddad had time to work since he seemed to be heading into town several times a week to meet his cronies at the Java Café, and then there were his poker nights. He even mentioned a history and biography book club at the library for seniors.

"You're really drinking lattes?" he roused himself to demand.

"Some young trendy barista home from college made me something called a caramel macchiato. Couldn't believe it, but she's Daniel's granddaughter so I couldn't say no. Now it's my go-to drink."

All three of them stared at their granddad, who tore off another hunk of chapati and chewed it thoughtfully. "I think I finally found a vice," he confessed.

Beck's fork clattered on the table.

"You're messing with us," Bodhi declared.

"Thought we could go out for a coffee after chores one morning this week," Granddad said, looking at all three of them. "You can treat," he said pointing at Beck, "and explain what fool thing you did to upset Ashni." His granddad had finally invited the elephant in the room into the conversation.

Beck winced, opened his mouth to defend himself, and at his granddad's glare, closed it again.

"Bowen will think of a plan to fix it, and you—" he smiled at Bodhi "—can think of a way to entertain my three daughters and keep them out of my hair and in yours instead."

"No thanks," Bodhi said, pushing his chair back to saunter to the stove to fix a plate of seconds. "I don't even know why they're coming. Especially during the rodeo. The moms are allergic to all things ranch, and my mama hasn't seen me ride a bull or rope since my junior rodeo days. Said it made her feel faint and doubt my sanity."

"Heck, me too." Granddad laughed. "But I do like to

watch you boys test fate and wrestle the beasts. Does the Ballantyne name proud."

Bodhi sat back down again and dug into his food.

"I'll miss all that." Granddad's deep rumble of a voice was almost an afterthought as he soaked up the last of his chicken masala with his last remaining chapati.

They'd already eaten through a third of the stack in one meal.

"We're still competing in the rodeo, Granddad," Bodhi said.

Silence met that statement.

"The moms are going to help with the Ballantyne Bash this year," Beck said into the awkward silence.

"They're probably a little nostalgic and wanting to have a last glimpse at their childhood home."

All three Ballantyne cousins paused mid bite following their granddad's statement. A large chunk of flavorful chicken freshly balanced on Bodhi's fork splatted back on his plate.

Granddad took another hearty bite of chicken and chewed thoughtfully. "Feeling the same way myself."

Beck forced himself to swallow. "Granddad, what's got you feeling nostalgic?" he asked cautiously. He wasn't actually falling in with the moms' plans, was he? An old folks' home? Assisted living? A condo? He doubted his granddad had even seen a condo.

"Well, you know—" he looked at them each in the eyes "—I'm not getting any younger."

With his wiry build, booming voice, full head of thick, salt-and-pepper hair that grew back from his strong, square, high forehead, and his dark brows that framed piecing blue eyes shining with command and life, Ben Ballantyne looked full of life and vigor.

"You all got your lives and dreams. My girls are all settled in Denver. None of you seem intent on settling down anytime soon. The legacy a ranch offers can be a gift or a burden. For me it's been both. Thought I'd try something new while I still can," he announced. "I'm thinking about selling the ranch."

Chapter Three

"He's messing with us." Beck leaned against the battered bar of Marietta's iconic Grey's Saloon and took the bottle of beer Bowen handed him. He'd been hit from all sides and was ready to swing—metaphorically—at anything.

"Definitely having a go with us," Bodhi said, but his voice that always rang with certainty had hollowed out.

Bowen palmed his beer with both hands as if in prayer. He looked down at the bottle. Usually, Granddad came out with them to Grey's for their Sunday night ritual their first night back.

Tonight, after his announcement, he'd waved them off, settled into his recliner, and put on a baseball game.

"I'm not sure," Bowen finally said.

"Maybe he needs the money. I mean, if he wanted to do something else with his life—" Beck spoke the words slowly because they felt like a foreign language in his mouth "—he'd need cash. He's land rich, not cash rich. It's his ranch to sell. The moms don't want it."

"Any of us would help him," Bodhi said. "We've all got plenty saved."

"But he wouldn't let us," Bowen said.

"You think the moms finally wore him down?" Beck asked.

His voice was so loaded with bitterness, it was shocking it didn't take a physical presence and sit down next to him.

"Can't imagine him caving to their constant demands. I never will," Bodhi vowed. "My mom is still yakking about me bringing home some smart, sweet girl and starting to churn out the kids. As if. Hand to God, that will never, ever happen." Bodhi held his right hand high and then, as if to punctuate his promise, he did a little trick with his thumb that Beck had never been able to master and flipped off his bottle cap, caught it, and spun it into the trash can right near the elbow of Jason Grey, the owner of the family-run bar.

He tipped his beer in Jason's irritated direction and drank deep. Grey's Saloon was an institution in Marietta. It had been the first building in town, a saloon that still had the balcony where, in the 1800s, the soiled doves had walked and watched and tempted the copper miners and cowboys and gamblers to spend their hard-earned cash. The Greys had always owned the saloon, only now it was one of the more respectable bars in town.

"Never say never," Bowen softly said, still not looking up from his beer.

"Never! Ever! Marriage is a beast that will claw out your innards," Bodhi called out. "Right, Jason?"

Jason, whose wife had left him and his daughters years ago and never come back, turned away, disgruntled as ever, and continued to make the Grey's Saloon signature pink cocktail for a boisterous table filled with young and attractive—in a high-maintenance style—women, who clearly seemed to be celebrating something. Likely bridal, judging from the askew veil one of them wore.

"That's a little harsh," Beck objected almost automatically, defending Ashni, girlfriends, and relationships everywhere.

"Right," Bodhi tipped his beer in his direction. "Don't see a ring on your finger."

Beck recoiled. What was wrong with everyone today?

"If my mom wanted me to marry, she shouldn't have ridden my ass so hard growing up with her litany of 'where you going, what are you doing, who are you with, when will you be home?'" Bodhi did an uncanny imitation of his mother. "Up in my business every second. Trying to dig into my head like it was a cheeseball at a Christmas party. Always going on about my feelings. Making me take drug tests for no reason except her own paranoia. I'm an athlete, not a stoner. If I tried to close my bedroom door, she freaked out probably thinking I was going to be like my father and off myself. So no. Never, ever giving any woman a chance to run me to the ground and stand on my back with a stiletto digging into my spine."

Wanna bet? was on the tip of Beck's tongue—a reflex. And from the glint in Bowen's eyes, he was thinking the same thing. Bets and challenges and one-upping each other. It was their thing. But tonight he kept his mouth shut. He wasn't feeling any of their usual camaraderie.

The day had utterly sucked. Jerry's stunt. Blowing a lead. His mom's call. Ashni texting that she was going to stay in town. Not taking his calls. Then his granddad's casual announcement that he was thinking of selling the ranch. His world just felt imploded.

Marietta was his happy place. Their happy place. What were they going to do if it was gone?

Uncharacteristically, Bodhi swore and took another deep swallow of his beer.

We're all off. Trying not to show it.

Two booths, crammed with women dressed for a serious night out, all watched them avidly.

Bit like being on stage. Or in a zoo. Beck was uncomfortable. He'd had his fair share of female attention over the years. But it was Bodhi who was movie-star handsome, like Brad Pitt when he'd first jumped into films. Bodhi had some sort of magic magnetic charisma that radiated off him. When he entered a room, women noticed. And they didn't look or walk away.

Beck had always lived a little vicariously through the attention Bodhi received and effortlessly wielded.

Bowen had the silent brooding down that women always wanted to peel back. Beck had never understood how Bowen could pick up a woman without saying much.

Tonight, though, it seemed like none of them wanted female attention. They needed to figure out a way to save their granddad from their moms' endless scheming. Beck just couldn't believe that the man who had practically raised them every summer and holiday to be stewards of the land would walk away from his home, his history, his legacy.

And he had to make things right with Ash.

Without thinking, he pulled out his phone.

Nothing.

"Take a night off," Bodhi growled. "For once in your life. She's given you a gift. Unwrap it." Bodhi indicated the display of bridesmaids. "Slip your leash."

Beck ignored him.

"Pick one. I'll help." Bodhi smiled and made eye contact with each woman before draining his beer.

"Hell no," Beck said and turned to Bowen. "Going out tonight was a bad idea."

"Gives us a place to talk if someone can keep his jeans zipped for twenty minutes," Bowen said. "We need a plan."

"I was just trying to help Beck up his game." Bodhi plunked his empty on the counter and indicated to the scowling Jason that they wanted another round, although Bowen had yet to open his first beer.

"Let me get this straight, you both are going with the theory that the old man's pulling our chain?" Bodhi demanded. "That this is some kind of game to him?"

"It's possible," Bowen mused.

Beck's tension cranked because Bowen was the most levelheaded, analytical person he knew. If he was worried, it was time to worry.

"So, if it's a game…" Bodhi swung around to face the

room and his arms stretched like wings along the bar. His lazy sprawl was definitely noted. The women in the two booths all turned as one and stared. Several preened.

Beck nearly swore. The last thing they needed tonight of all nights when Beck felt like he was crawling out of his skin was Bodhi hip-deep in flirt.

"Let's play a little game with him." Bodhi took the three beers Jason had plunked down loudly, popped off the tops, and handed them out. "Drink up," he advised, his eyes—so like their grandfather's piercing blue with a darker navy ring around the iris that was startling and a little unnerving—glinted with purpose. "I've thought of a fun game we could play."

Bowen finally took a swig of his beer. "We need a plan, not a game."

"We're Ballantynes. We make a game of everything. Hell—" Bodhi took another deep pull "—Granddad taught us how to compete practically out of our mothers' wombs."

It was harder to hear with the bar filling up. The music kicked up louder and the pool games were in full swing.

"He's not selling." Beck wanted the words to be real.

"Not if we can persuade him to stay put." Bodhi grinned. "I say we call his bluff."

"How?"

"What's Granddad all about?"

Beck would have said the ranch.

"What? I'm the only one who listened up in college? Took a psych class?" Bodhi taunted them. "Family. Granddad is all about family."

Bowen and Beck nodded.

Bodhi slapped his hands together and rubbed them vigorously. "Who's in?"

"Me."

"Me."

Beck and Bowen spoke in unison.

Bodhi's eyes glinted with a wicked light.

"What's the game?" Beck and Bowen both demanded.

"Marriage," Bodhi said flatly.

"Marriage isn't a game," Beck objected.

"It can be." Bodhi jangled with unleashed tension. "We can all play. We'll call it the Rodeo Brides Game."

"You were just hand to God-ing it that you would never, ever get married," Beck reminded him, although that pronouncement alone should doom Bodhi to getting hitched by the end of the Copper Mountain Rodeo.

"I won't. But I can bring a fiancée home to the Ballantyne Bash."

"You're not even dating," Beck scoffed.

"What's dating got to do with it? The winner of the game is the first one to bring home a future bride to Granddad."

"And then what?" Bowen asked skeptically.

"Granddad can stop worrying that the Ballantyne legacy is in peril. He'll know the next generation of Ballantynes is on the way. The moms won't be able to sway him to sell."

"What are the rules?" Beck crossed his arms. This was

going to be good. Not.

"First one to get engaged wins, but Granddad has to believe it."

"What's the prize?" Bowen asked.

Beck glared at Bowen. He wasn't actually considering this stupidity? But he was. Bodhi looked lit from within, radiating an 'I dare you' that had gotten them in trouble more than a few times over the years.

Bowen's eyes were flinty and narrowed. A muscle in his jaw ticked.

A recklessness swarmed over Beck as his competitive nature, the one that had always driven him to keep up and then try to surpass his cousins, kicked in.

"Plum Hill," Beck said feeling reckless and wanting to stop the madness.

"I CAN'T BELIEVE this week is finally here." Ashni plopped her suitcase, computer bag and large tote with her art supplies near the saddle-colored leather sofa. "I have been so excited, done so much research and keep changing my lesson plans."

Sky Wilder laughed. "So you keep saying. Careful, I might try to persuade you to stay." She hefted two remaining bags of groceries onto the counter. "After that Punjabi cooking class you effortlessly staged at Three Trees for me, Walker, Talon and Tucker, I don't think any of my sisters-in-law are going to let you leave town."

"I'm on board with Sky's plan," Walker, who owned the two carriage-style apartments with her husband, said. "This apartment is available beyond the week if you want. My husband just uses it for his team when they come to edit footage for their Ghost Quest Specials or his documentaries about the raptor rescue. Since the baby's due any day now, we don't have anything scheduled for a while so I too will try to convince you to stay."

"I might let you," Ashni said, feeling both bold and nervous.

Was she really going to upend her entire life on a whim?

The dread that had been vying with anticipation since she'd sent in her resignation notched higher, making her tummy lurch and her heart pound.

Walker gave her a quick tour of the spacious studio apartment above a massive four-car garage and showed her how to work the Murphy bed and pull down the table built into the front facing when the bed was in the wall. The bathroom was nice with a soaking tub that was as unexpected as it was welcome. Traveling with Beck hadn't yielded many times to relax in a bath with candles and bath bombs—just quick, tepid showers in the shower-stall-sized bathroom in his rig.

"This is nice," Ashni said her eyes taking in the spacious room.

"The other apartment is rented out to my replacement at the Graff Hotel for the year," Walker finished. "Langston

Carr. She grew up in Marietta but left for college and then worked in event planning for a huge firm in Missoula and Helena. I'm taking a whole year off with this monkey." Her hands rested on her large, rounded belly. "Calum is going to work on a documentary in the spring, and we'll be able to travel with him."

Her face glowed, and Ashni felt a stab of envy that she tried to shove aside. She'd vowed to give herself this week to start making plans for the future she wanted, Beck or no Beck. And to do that, she had to stop thinking about him all the time.

She definitely didn't feel ready to talk to him, and that alone was making her feel strange and unmoored. Beck had been her best friend and confidant since high school. She shared everything with him. And now she hadn't even called him back after his flurry of voicemails and texts. At least he knew she was okay since she'd visited his granddad and cooked him his favorite meal.

Ben hadn't asked about Beck, he'd just watched her cook, his kind gaze so like Bodhi's it was eerie. The Indian cooking lesson had been a balm she hadn't expected. She'd fretted about not fixing Ben his favorite meal when she and Sky had been at Monroe's grocery store, and Sky had suggested going out to the ranch and cooking, and then she'd texted her family, and there had been a lot of enthusiastic yesses. Only one of Sky's sisters-in-law hadn't been able to attend.

Marietta would be a wonderful town to settle in.

And Beck would be in Marietta eventually. Maybe then they could start again. Or he'd find…

Stop thinking about Beck.

It was supposed to be a Beck-free week. Another vow she'd made on the plane. But she would have to tell him that—that she wanted a break. And she didn't feel ready for that at all.

Coward.

Definitely.

"You two should go out and have some fun," Walker urged. "There's a band at FlintWorks. The bar at the Graff will probably be pretty full. Shane plays a couple of sets on her upright and sings. Dang, she's good. Calum and I often go on Sundays to hear her, but I feel too big to move and just want to soak in the bath. Thanks for the cooking class today, Ash. You have my cell if you need anything."

Walker left. Sky had finished putting away the groceries.

"Let's go out," Sky said. "Kane's with the kids so I'm going to relish my freedom. I am not going to ask you about Beck, but if you want to talk about him, I'm here," Sky said, her beautiful blue eyes warm with sympathy.

"Thanks. I have some things to figure out about him and the future," Ashni said. "But I don't have anything sorted."

And she was a little freaked out that she'd impulsively applied for a job without even discussing it with Beck. Or Reeva. Or her parents. Nothing might come of it. She'd been out of school for a while although she'd kept current with online seminars and journals, and she'd participated in a few research projects and had volunteered with children's programs at hospitals in the cities where the rodeo visited.

I probably won't get it.

What if I get an interview?

The questions wrestled one another in her brain.

"So is that a yes to going out?" Sky bounced on her feet.

Ash was exhausted. Bone-tired. But she didn't want to be alone with her thoughts.

"I'm up for it." She forced energy into her voice hoping it soaked into her body and brain. She checked her Apple watch. If they stopped by Harry's House first, Beck would most likely be gone from Grey's, so she wouldn't run into him there or on Main Street. Ben never stayed out late. Rancher hours were long, and Beck and his cousins were all hard workers. When they were on the ranch, they did their best to help their granddad out with chores and projects to take some of the load off of him.

"I need to get out of my head."

"And maybe out of something else." Sky shimmied playfully. "Sometimes a little flirting can do wonders to wake dumb cowboys out of their idiotic stupor."

"We aren't talking about Beck."

"Who said anything about Beck?" Sky asked innocently.

A little devil—one she didn't know she had—tapped Ash's shoulder.

"Let's go to Grey's."

He'd probably be gone. But what if he wasn't?

"Plum Hill? No. Way," Bowen said.

"Why not? It's my favorite part of the ranch," Beck countered. The thrill of competing against his cousins crawled through his blood instinctively.

"Plum Hill is the favorite spot for all of us," Bowen said.

"Then what better to have on the line?" Beck demanded. "Bottoms up," he drained his second beer, unusual for him. Beck felt untethered, and he watched Bodhi as if that would somehow help him divine where his cousin was going with this game idea. Bodhi had launched and misfired many schemes before but nothing this radical.

"No," Bodhi said firmly. "Not Plum Hill. Not a physical prize for any of us." He shook his head. "The win is Granddad choosing to stay in his home, on the ranch."

"Or telling us why he's really thinking of selling so we can help out if he needs it," Bowen's baritone cut through the noise of the bar. "Not financial gain for anyone. Not Plum Hill."

That settled Beck somewhat. He and his cousins were inherently competitive with each other, but the ranch was sacred. Family. Still, he wasn't sure if Bodhi had thought this 'game' through. Was alcohol talking as much as Bodhi? "So, you're just going to wow some girl this week. Bring her home. Wow Granddad by dropping to one knee and break both their hearts when you ride off on tour again?"

Beck couldn't believe this. Sure, Bodhi was a player, but he didn't have a mean bone in his body.

"Seriously, how long does your little charade last—to the end of the rodeo or the bash? You're not really going to go through with the engagement, are you?"

"I was hoping you'd go through with it." Bodhi clapped Beck's shoulder hard enough to hurt. "You at least have a girl, and before you give me any more grief about my plan or my lifestyle, look in the mirror."

Beck looked at the large, tarnished mirror behind the bar. It had been there longer than he'd been alive. Probably longer than Granddad had walked Three Tree pastures.

"Not literally," Bodhi said. "You think I'd break some girl's heart? Never. That's your specialty."

"What's that supposed to mean?"

"You've been stringing Ash along for years. Years, Beck. Cut her loose. Let her find some happiness."

"She is happy," Beck grit out.

"Then why is she not here?" Bodhi demanded, then he turned to Bowen. "So it's you and me."

Bowen didn't answer, but Beck could tell he was thinking about it. This was a disaster.

"You can't cut me out."

"You think you can play?" Bodhi challenged.

Beck's chest felt tight. He couldn't play some game with Ashni.

Bodhi didn't look at him. His calculated gaze swept the room. "Granddad's happiness is on the line."

"You're going to find a bride in a week?" Beck demanded incredulously.

"I can find one tonight." Bodhi looked straight ahead at the two booths of tipsy women.

"You can't."

"Can."

"You won't," Bowen said firmly. "You're a player, but you'd never take advantage of some drunk woman. That would be cruel."

"What is cruel about promising a lovely lady some of me?" Bodhi grinned.

"You're bluffing." Beck was certain.

A muscle ticked in Bodhi's perfect jawline that many women and too many photographers had rhapsodized about.

"Bet you'd both jump into the game if I make the first play," he challenged.

"One play is all you got," Beck said. "You'd never stick around long enough to get her number so how are you going to get engaged?"

"I stick what I need to stick," Bodhi said. "You two in for some wooing this week or what?"

Beck felt the words like a physical blow—his lost lead today. "You're going to hook up with some random woman and ask her to marry you in a week?" Beck angrily raised his voice above the music and swelling crowd. It was packed for a Sunday for sure, and two checks of his phone and he still hadn't heard from Ash. Where was she even staying?

Bodhi looked over at Bowen. "I know you're in."

Again Bowen didn't respond, but Beck could tell his cousin was interested. He was too still, his bluish-gray eyes narrowed, and his jaw cranked tight.

"This is crazy!"

"It's fun," Bodhi countered. "Besides, we're not going to marry the poor girls. We just need to squire them around this week and during the rodeo so they don't look like one-night stands. Take her to dinner. Horse ride at the ranch. Dance at the steak dinner. Arrive at the Ballantyne Bash looking stupidly besotted. Voila! We will have bought ourselves some time. Granddad will think the next generation's knocking on the door, and the moms will sulk off back to Denver and give all of us men some breathing room."

"What if Granddad wants to sell the ranch?" It was a kick in the gut to say it.

"He doesn't," Bodhi said, but his voice lacked its usual easy confidence, and he didn't look either of them in the eye. "But one of us needs to pin him down. If he needs money, he can have mine."

"And mine," Bowen and Beck stated at the same time.

"And if Granddad needs help, one of us peels off the tour. We can flip for it."

"You are not going to find a woman who will agree to a fake engagement."

"Watch and learn, little cuz. It will be easy."

"This whole game is stupid," Bowen finally said. "Beck's got us lapped. He's got Ashni."

"So you are in." Bodhi flipped his hat back a little on his

head with a forefinger and smirked. "Like I said, Beck can't play."

"Why the hell not?"

"Ashni's off-limits."

"How can I play if she's off-limits?" Beck demanded. He couldn't show up at the ranch with another woman and be believable. Just the idea of it turned his stomach.

"Because it's a game." Bodhi got in his face. "Ashni's real. You don't get to play with what's real."

"So it's up to you and me to save Granddad and the ranch," Bowen said, already cutting Beck out.

"Exactly."

"Like hell," Beck objected.

"Let's review all the rules." Bowen turned toward Bodhi, ignoring Beck. "We both have a week to find a woman who will agree to play along and get fake engaged to us by the Ballantyne Bash?"

"A week," Bodhi scoffed. "I'm going to find her tonight. I'll be engaged before you get a date. I'll be engaged at the steak dinner."

"I'll be engaged before it starts." Bowen took a last swallow of his beer and put it down with a definitive clunk on the bar. "I'm in."

"This is madness," Beck objected.

"Makes you feel alive, doesn't it?" Bodhi was already scanning the room. "Or it would if you were in the game."

"I'm in." Beck's blood surged making him reckless. "New rule. The proposal has to be during the bash in front of the moms and Granddad. And after, we ask them to rate the most romantic or creative."

"Hell no," Bowen burst out. "I'm not making a public spectacle of myself in front of all of Marietta!"

"You're on." Bodhi signaled for another beer and then his eyes locked on a tall, slender beauty with flowing red hair who'd just entered Grey's and stopped short, her back pressed against the double doors. "Public proposal slitting our wrists and throats and bleeding out our hearts publicly." He smirked at Bowen. "This is going to be fun."

Bowen turned away, his jaw set.

Bodhi laughed, but his gaze had never deviated from the woman who'd just entered Grey's.

"Dibs," Bodhi said softly, in full hunter mode. "Meet my future bride."

Beck gaped at his cousin and then looked back at the unsuspecting woman. Should he warn her?

"Watch and learn." Bodhi strode over to the woman whose hair glinted fire from the bar's lighting. Her lush lips parted, and her eyes widened as Bodhi swept off his hat and did a little bow that should have looked ridiculous but somehow worked. He gently took her hand and spoke to her, indicating his recently vacated barstool.

"One day a woman is going to slap him," Bowen said amused, his good temper restored.

"Not holding my breath," Beck muttered. "You're not really going to take that challenge, are you?"

"Never backed down yet," Bowen said.

"This is crazy. You're just going to pick some random woman in a bar and..." He could hardly put the challenge into words.

"No. Not here. Somewhere else."

"Where?"

"Don't know. The opportunity will arise. I'll just seize it."

Bodhi had seized his. He helped the woman sit on the barstool then he casually leaned against the bar and introduced his cousins.

She was model-gorgeous and stared into Bodhi's eyes like he had the answer to questions she hadn't yet thought of.

"I'm outta here," Beck said. He and his cousins had done some crazy stuff over the years, but this was bouncing on a whole new level.

Beck pulled his phone from his pocket and walked toward the exit when a tall, curvaceous blonde from the bridal party stopped him. He'd felt her staring a hole in him since he'd arrived.

"Are you a real cowboy?" she asked, her fingertips skimming over the belt buckle he'd won today. "A rodeo cowboy?" Her voice was soft, her hair so blonde it glowed. Her gaze was bold, assessing, and admiring.

She was also one pink drink beyond tipsy.

"Yes, ma'am," he said politely. "Let me get you back to your friends."

Her fingers continued to caress his belt buckle. He caught her hand as it drifted lower.

"Do you taste as sweet as you talk?"

He wasn't touching that.

"Excuse me, ma'am. I need to…"

"You are sex on a stick. Say it again. The ma'am thing."

"I think I better get you back to your friends, ma'am. Or call you a cab or…" He looked for help, but Bodhi looked away from him—probably laughing, the bastard.

And Bowen looked amused and turned to talk to Luke Wilder, a former rodeo cowboy from the tour who now lived locally and raised bucking bulls and broncs with his wife and family.

"I'm Shauna. Will you be my cowboy tonight?"

"No, ma'am, I'm taken."

"The good ones always are. Dance with me. One dance, please. It took me this long to get my courage up to talk to you. My twin sister's getting married this week and I'm single. Everyone will laugh at me if you walk away."

Damn.

"Would you care to dance, Shauna?" he asked.

Her smile was bright but goofy, and he hoped he could get in the dance before she puked. This never happened to Bodhi. Never. Ever.

"I learned how to two-step online." She pressed tightly against him, one hand jammed down his back pocket, the other hand was around his neck and in his hair. "And we had a lesson this week as part of the bridal activities." She draped herself all over him. "Show me how it's done, cowboy," she said throatily.

This was not how it was done. Beck kept trying to politely keep some distance, but she kept pressing up against him and doing a rather suggestive hip grind. He could feel the press of her breasts—braless in her bright red and white sundress.

"There's usually more distance with the steps so I can turn you," Beck said more than once, but Shauna wasn't having any of that.

He'd never been so relieved when a song ended. He disentangled himself to urge her to return to her table, when another song started up, this one a Chris Stapleton ballad, and one dance became two as Shauna began to sing and snuggle closer. Her lips brushed his neck. Beck kept his hold on her loose, but for the most part it was more wrestling than dancing. He began to two-step them toward the door, determined to either get her back to her friends or call her a cab.

"I'm staying at the Graff," she said, digging her spiked heels into the already abused floors of Grey's. "I have my own room. I'm the maid of honor. No expense spared. Want to join me?"

What did she take him for, a cowboy escort?

"I can walk you to the hotel," he said. But that was all he was doing.

She laughed and dragged him toward her table. He needed to make a quick escape. Shauna picked up a drink from the tray the waitress was delivering and started to slurp.

"This is my cowboy," she shouted. "I'm taking him back

to my room," she told her friends, who cheered.

Hell no!

"Ma'am." He tried to extricate himself from her unexpectedly tenacious grip.

How had this happened to him? Bodhi was definitely laughing. He even toasted him with his beer, double bastard. Bowen scowled as if Beck had instigated this disaster.

"I'm going to ride a cowboy," Shauna bragged, still holding a drink high in her hand as she weaved back toward the door. One hand still gripped his belt and buckle.

"Coming though. I got me a hottie," Shauna shouted as she pulled them through the double swinging doors.

Shauna stood in front of Grey's double doors, blocking them and faced him. "You are hotter than the sun. And so strong. Did you know there are six hundred and fifty skeletal muscles in the human body? I bet you exercise each one." She stumbled into him and tipped her drink, dousing his white shirt with pink.

"Oops! Wet T-shirt contest. You win." She leaned into him to lick his shirt.

Worst night of his life ever. "Let's get you back to your hotel." Using his body, he moved her the rest of the way out of Grey's, steadying her by keeping his hands on her shoulders. Was he going to have to carry her?

Once on the sidewalk, he came face-to-face with Ashni, who stood with Sky Wilder, waiting to get into Grey's. Both had nearly identical expressions of shock on their faces, and Ashni blinked several times like she did when she was trying to suppress strong emotion or process something confusing.

Damn. His night just tanked worse.

"Uhhhh, Ash. This isn't what it looks like," he stammered in horror stepping away from Shauna, who weaved and then faced the two women.

"You wasted no time," Ashni said.

"No. I didn't. I mean…I'm not…" Never as quick or glib as Bodhi, Beck grasped at an explanation.

"Hey, he's mine tonight. Find your own cowboy," Shauna slurred.

"No thanks." Ash brushed by them both. "I'm done with cowboys, especially this one. Enjoy."

Ash swept through the door of Grey's linking arms with Sky Wilder, who threw in a silky hair toss and glare his way.

"I think I'm going to be sick," Shauna announced.

Beck already was.

He stared at the doors as they swung shut. He had to get in there. He had to explain. But Ash's accusation was ludicrous. How could she think he'd pick up a woman a few hours after she left? And she hadn't even left, not really. They hadn't broken up.

He wouldn't know how.

He stared at the weaving Shauna, loath to touch her but not able to leave her on the street in this condition. Would it be better to put her in his truck to make better time or walk her to the hotel, hoping she'd sober up some?

"Need some help, cowboy?" Bowen came out.

"Now you ride to my rescue? Ash is about to castrate

me."

"Don't let me stand in her way. I'll take…?"

"Shauna, I think. Or Sheila?" Beck couldn't remember. Seeing Ashni had scrambled his brain.

"You're cute." Shauna looked up at Bowen, clearly having no loyalty, and relief coursed through Beck.

"So I've heard," Bowen said. "But I think it was just once and a rumor my mother started."

Shauna laughed so hard she snorted. "OMG. You're funny."

"You're wasted on the rodeo," Beck told his cousin. "Maybe Comedy Central. Cowboy stand-up." It felt a little better now that Bowen had his back.

"Go get your girl."

"I intend to." Beck squared his shoulders and shoved open the doors.

Chapter Four

Ashni perched on a barstool that Luke Wilder, Sky's brother-in-law, had vacated for her. She angled her body toward the bar. She was not going to look at the swinging doors. She wasn't. She didn't care that Beck had replaced her within a couple of hours with a vivacious, gorgeous, tall, curvy blonde who drank Grey's signature pink drink and probably giggled like a middle school girl.

She was fine being single!

That's what this week, maybe a year, maybe forever was all about. Time to plan for a future—without Beck, who'd seized the first opportunity to get horizontal with the first willing woman. The memory of the hook-up questions he'd asked Bodhi mocked her, and, no, those were not tears stinging her eyes!

Totally unlike him—or so she'd thought. He never looked at women when they were out, and they'd looked at him. A lot. Especially on the tour.

She'd wanted some space. Looked like she'd got it. Permanently.

Ashni pulled herself out of her slouch—her former *Shastriya Devesh* instructor would be horrified at her slumping posture. She could practically hear the scold from states away.

"What can I get you two?" Luke asked politely.

"Club soda with lime," she said while Sky ordered a whiskey.

"Wild woman," Ashni teased.

"Make that two whiskeys, Luke," Sky said all saucy. "I'm going to teach Ashni how to shoot whiskey so she can look badass cowgirl when her idiot man comes charging in hangdog muttering some dumb explanation."

"To be fair," Luke began, "he—"

"I don't want to hear it," Ashni interrupted. Seeing Beck with a woman who was the total opposite of her—stumbling drunk from a bar—would make it easier to ignore him this week. Make that forever.

"He seemed pretty occupied," she added, aiming for casual, but her voice sounded raw. She would not cry. Instead she wanted to smack that shocked look off his face. And maybe kick him in the balls with the toe of the new boots she'd bought with Sky today.

She'd had such a surreal day. Watching Beck dodge Jerry's nosy questions on TV and having to make light of it in front of her parents and family. Her rash resignation and job application. The fun shopping with Sky and making dinner for Ben without any of 'the boys.' Ashni felt like she'd just been put on a spin cycle.

She could feel Bodhi watching her, trying to get her attention, practically willing her to look or walk over, but he was also chatting up a beautifully rich, auburn-haired woman.

Men.

She'd been to Grey's Saloon many times with Beck and his cousins, but she'd only had eyes for one man. And he for her. But now that she was newly single, she should at least pretend to look around and be interested in other men.

"Here, try this. Look happy."

"What?"

"He's here." Sky firmly put a tumbler of whiskey in her hand.

Ashni's heart jumped to her throat. Beck was back? With or without his tipsy conquest? She so wasn't going to look.

OMG, I'm in middle school again.

"But I ordered a..."

"Whiskey will look cooler," Sky interrupted. "Toss it back and throw yourself into the burn," Sky advised. "Just don't toss it in his face. This is my brother-in-law Laird's top-shelf. And if your man's acting stupid, he's not worth the good stuff. Besides—" Sky swung her long hair behind her and smiled, her blue eyes alight with mischief "—Jason will kick you out if you act up, and he has a long memory. Luke's been tossed out." Sky needled her brother-in-law.

Luke slid the club soda in front of Ashni as well. "Thank you for the reminder, little sister, but Colt was tossed as well, and we're both back in Jason's good graces."

"As if there is such a thing," Sky said. "At least pretend to sip. Laird finally convinced Jason to give him a trial month with the whiskey to see what patrons think. Choking on it or having the top-shelf tossed at a cowboy, no matter how badly he deserves it, will not make the impression Laird wants. Well, considering it's Laird, maybe that is an impression he could get behind. Ignore Beck. Act cool. Make him sweat. Use his F-up as creative fodder."

"I'm going to tell my little brother Kane his wife has a mean streak a mile wide," Luke said. "Ladies, enjoy your night of cruelty toward men and acting cool." Luke pulled out his phone and texted before walking away to join another group of cowboys.

Ashni couldn't breathe, much less act cool. Sky was acting like this was fun, and Ashni found herself utterly unable to enter the spirit of the game. Games were more the Ballantyne thing. One would think she would have picked up some skills after so many years. But she did have a lot of acting experience to draw from.

"Showtime," she murmured and pretended to take a sip of the whiskey. Even the fumes made her eyes water. Definitely the whiskey, not what was going down with Beck and pink drink swilling—judging by the pink splattered on Beck's shirt—blonde.

And then he was here. Even before she saw him, she felt him. And smelled him: orange, cedar, cinnamon and something that was uniquely Beck. She couldn't help herself. She closed her eyes and inhaled deeply.

"Ash, I can explain." The deep timbre of his voice tingled her ears, and the buzz went down to her toes.

She felt herself melt—melt with longing and forgiveness and…stupid girl. Her eyes snapped open. Not happening. Be strong. She didn't want her life to revolve around Beck, and she couldn't throw herself back into his arms the moment he got within touching range. Besides, the pink splash on his white shirt and the way the shirt's wet spot clung to his well-defined chest reminded her of what he'd been doing and with whom.

She thought of something snarky to say—well, bitchy, really—but instead closed her eyes and sniffed at the whiskey in what she hoped looked like appreciation. At least the whiskey drowned out Beck's scent a little.

Beck could do whatever he wanted as long as it was without her.

"No explanation necessary." She looked up into his eyes, bracing herself to act cool—whatever that looked like in Sky's opinion. But the open misery in his expression made her heart squeeze.

"Hi." Sky smiled. "I'm Sky. This is my friend, Ashni."

The misery morphed to confusion. "Yeah, I know," he said.

"You in town for the rodeo?" Sky asked a little flirtatiously.

What was Sky playing at? She knew who Beck was. Ashni pretended to take another tiny sip of the whiskey. "You're right—this is top-shelf."

"You hate whiskey." Beck's blue gaze continued to bore a hole in her soul. "Besides…" He leaned into her. Her breath tangled in her throat and her heart hammered. "You didn't even taste it."

"I did."

"Prove it," he softly challenged and somehow her heart kicked up harder.

"I don't have to prove anything to you," she said.

"True." His gaze dropped to her mouth, and her lips tingled. "Because I know that you didn't take a sip."

"Whiskey's my new favorite drink," she declared.

"Then maybe you should take a sip, cowgirl." He pressed his thumb on her bottom lip. "Or you could share."

"I don't share," she said quickly.

"Me neither," he whispered in her ear. His breath was warm; fluttered her hair and caressed her cheek. Her heart flipped. Was he flirting with her?

She palmed the whiskey, needing something to hold that wasn't Beck.

"What's your top money-making event?" Sky rolled her own glass in her palms, warming it.

Ashni looked between the two of them. Was she supposed to be taking notes? Was this creative fodder? "You look as though you like to tie things up," Sky said innocently, but the sparkle in her eyes was wicked.

Had the girl gone crazy? She didn't know Sky all that well, but she was a young metals artist with her professional reputation on a steep upward trajectory. She was married to a husband who clearly adored her, and she was a mother with three young children. She was also on the board of

Harry's House and part of a large, almost dynastic family. Should flirty game player be added to the list?

Ashni definitely needed to take notes—not for Beck—but for the future.

"I do enjoy roping. It gives me great pleasure." Beck drawled out the last word and angled his body closer to Ashni's. Her body lit up. Ignited. Like they weren't in a public place loud with conversation, laughing, country music, and the crack of pool balls.

A game! Ashni practically slapped her palm against her forehead. Of course. Sky was playing with Beck. Her husband was a recently retired top-tier bull rider. All rodeo cowboys thrived on challenge.

And I've been a really sure thing for a long time.

"How are your moves, cowboy?" Sky challenged. "You any good on the dance floor?"

"I can hold my own." Beck's hand slid across Ashni's shoulders and down her back to rest lightly on her hip. She couldn't help the shiver of awareness as goose bumps rose up to say "welcome home."

Stupid body.

"I'd love to give you a demonstration with your friend here." Beck smiled down at her. He mouthed, 'I missed you.'

Ashni was trapped in the heat of his blue gaze. No. This was not supposed to happen. She wasn't supposed to cave at the first challenge. How was she supposed to make this into a game? She didn't do games. Not ever.

And yet you fell in love with a man who is constantly en-

gaged in an "I can do better than you" challenge with his cousins.

"I was hoping for a more up-close and personal demonstration," Sky said.

"What?" Beck looked totally shocked. "With you? But…" He looked from Sky to her, almost pleading.

Ashni stifled the urge to laugh. It was fun to see Beck thrown off his game. And why shouldn't she play too? Sky was having fun, maybe punishing Beck a little for leaving a bar with a rather drunk blonde, but now that Ashni had processed the shock, she knew Beck wouldn't cheat or hook up with a woman who was drunk.

"That's not very polite, cowboy," she said. "My friend all but asked you to dance. You're not going to leave her hanging, are you?" She lifted the whiskey to her lips. "Besides, you bragged about your moves. I want to see them."

"Ashni?"

"You may not know this about me, but I like to watch."

Shock at her audacity flooded through her, and a surprised heat entered his gaze. Maybe she needed to dial it down a bit.

"I prefer first-hand experience." Sky's gaze was bold as it roved from Beck's face, down his body and back up again, slowly.

"Ahhhhh." Pink tinged his cheeks, which lightened Ashni's mood considerably. When had she become so serious? She was becoming a dud—always worrying about the future like her mom, never reveling in the moment anymore.

Beck took the whiskey from Ashni and took a healthy sip.

"Now you can taste it." He brushed his lips over hers, and it was all Ashni could do to hold off from tossing herself into his kiss. Beck lingered, his mouth barely touching hers.

"I'd love to dance," he said. "I'd just like to explain something to Ashni that happened but didn't happen. I haven't seen my girl for two weeks, and I want…"

"No." Ashni stood, making sure that her body brushed against Beck's, and she let her denim jacket slip down her shoulders so that they were bare. "You don't need to explain anything." She stood on tiptoes and whispered, letting her lips brush his clean-shaven jaw, "Dance with Sky. I want to watch."

The second flare of heat in his eyes nearly crumbled her resolve.

"I'll buy you a drink." She slipped her hand in his back pocket, spreading her fingers wide for a moment to curl them into his very prime, firm ass and then extracted his wallet. "On you," she said touching the top of her lip with her tongue—a move she'd read about in so many romances. Too obvious?

His regard focused on her mouth, and she felt like he almost kissed her again. Heat bloomed from her breasts to her core. No. She was supposed to be playing a flirtation game. Not falling under the spell she was clumsily trying to weave.

"I know what you like," she murmured.

"What I love," he corrected, fingers brushing hers.

For a moment she almost held on to him. It would be so easy. But no. She needed to walk on her own for a while. If Beck wanted to have a life with her, he had to love the woman she wanted to become, not just the one she'd been. She didn't want either of them to stay together out of habit.

"Enjoy your dance." She looked into his warm blue eyes that always reminded her of a lake in summer.

"I will." One finger stroked her cheek, and it took all her willpower not to lean into his hand. "But the dance later with you will be even sweeter."

Where was the air? How did she swallow?

"Maybe," she said angling her body away from him, making sure her bottom brushed his groin. She heard him hiss, and it felt like the sun rose in her chest.

"Bartender," she called out.

★

IT TOOK A lot of discipline to keep his attention focused on his dance partner, when he wanted to get back to Ash. She looked fantastic. She had sort of a mustard-colored, soft wrap dress he hadn't seen before. It was off the shoulder, exposing her silky dark skin, and it hugged her body and skimmed several inches above her knee. Where had she been hiding that dress? And did the bow at her waist hold the dress on or was it for show? A vision of him untying the dress and it puddling around her new cowboy boots suddenly left him needing to adjust himself.

Do not think of Ash naked. Or the dress.

"You do have a few moves," Sky teased. "But your attention needs some work."

"Sorry." Beck looked down into her upturned face. "I just..." He took her hand and spun Sky left in a tight circle and then right and then they two-stepped counterclockwise around the perimeter of the small dance floor. "Ashni's been away at a family wedding for a couple of weeks, and I really missed her."

And she hadn't answered his calls or returned his texts today.

Bodhi, like always, had been right. Something was very, very wrong.

And he had to fix it.

"Let her have fun tonight," Sky advised and then executed a smooth dance move that pulled his concentration off of Ashni, who was laughing at the bar with the Wilders.

"I want her to have fun," he said. "I just want it to be with me."

"Maybe she wants to be appreciated. Wooed." Sky executed a few more spin moves that should have been his to direct. "Eyes on me, cowboy."

"Sorry." He spun Sky around and they switched directions to execute another spin before moving around the floor again. She was light on her feet and easy to dance with, but he'd never felt less like dancing.

Was Ashni going to actually shoot whiskey?

He wanted to see that. And taste her lips after.

Luke and the other Wilder seemed to be encouraging her to try it. They each had shots in their hands now. Bodhi, leaning against the bar with the woman he'd corralled, also seemed to be talking his current conquest through the art of the whiskey shot. Kane Wilder strode through Grey's double doors. His gaze lit on his wife, and then he joined his brothers.

Perfect. Beck's squiring duties would surely be over. But just as the song ended, Ash did the shot, tipping her head back, exposing her graceful throat and pronounced collarbone that he loved to butterfly kiss as he undressed her. He was captivated. She'd cast a spell over him since he'd first seen her through the glass section of the high school music room door. Ash held her arms up in victory and laughed. She looked so vibrant in the historic bar. Alive. She hopped off the barstool and stomped her feet a few times.

"That was fire," she called out.

And he wanted to burn with her. Beck turned Sky toward the bar just as another song kicked in. Ash smiled and took Kane's hand as he led her onto the dance floor.

"Stuck with me." Sky laughed at his dilemma.

"What do you say we kick it up a notch?"

"You lead." Her lips tipped up in a smile. "That would require you paying attention."

"I can focus when I need to."

Sky looked over at her husband, smiled, and winked. He tipped his hat to her.

Beck loved to dance. But he rarely partnered anyone other than Ashni. It was strange and arousing to watch her move around the floor, grace, confidence with a little attitude. Kane smiled and chatted even as he maneuvered her through some showy turns. Beck got creative with Sky, and she seemed delighted, laughing when he rolled her across his back and then swung her around his front without missing a beat.

"You do have moves," she said. "When you need to play."

"Not everything's a game."

Like Bodhi's Rodeo Bride Game. How would that end in anything but disaster?

Bowen hadn't returned from the Graff.

Bodhi was still at the bar with the woman, now demonstrating the basic two-step, his hands light but definitely on her body as he guided her in place through the moves.

Were his cousins really going to go through with something so outrageous? And why had he jumped into the game instead of sitting on the sidelines for once? Everything inside of him shouted out a big fat no to that idea. But Granddad's happiness was on the line. And how would he persuade Ashni to play along when she was already upset with him?

The engagement would have to be real.

His breath seized in his lungs.

It wasn't as if everyone hadn't been expecting them to marry since they'd graduated college. But the revolving door of his mother's husbands during his childhood had been dizzying, and after his father moved on and started a new family, cutting Beck out of his life, and the first stepfather walked out after two years, Beck hadn't bothered getting to know any of the others or his bio dad.

He didn't want to be that man.

But he was going to have to go down on one knee in a far more public and showy proposal than would be to his liking, now that he'd egged his cousins on and upped the stakes.

And Ash would say yes. She'd been hinting at marriage for a while now. She'd asked him straight out last Christmas, and he'd barely dodged her question with a mumbled something followed by a lust-driven assault on her body to distract both her and him.

She'd be hurt if she thought he was playing a game—once again trying to outdo his cousins.

So it would be real. He tried to swallow the panic that scratched his throat, like he'd swallowed a Brillo pad.

"You look like you're doing calculus in your head."

"Kinda feels like," he admitted.

"I'll be rooting for you during the roping games," Sky stood on tiptoes and whispered. "Now go kiss and make up. You have my approval to woo my new friend."

"Kane's got his hands full."

Sky curtsied. "That's how he likes it."

Beck turned to Ash, his heart feeling like it would hop out of his chest. He hadn't been this nervous to ask her to dance since freshman year of high school. He swept off his hat.

"Ma'am, may I have the next dance?"

Ashni hesitated, biting down hard on her full, pouty lower lip, and Beck's heart felt like it skipped a beat. "Please," he added.

The music started up. Beck didn't recognize the song, but it didn't matter. As long as he could hold Ash in his arms, nothing else mattered.

"Please," he repeated and held out his hand. Ashni watched her friends dance off. Her shoulders dropped and alarm skittered through him.

"Whatever's wrong, we can fix it," he promised.

"I don't think you can, Beck," she said softly, but still she allowed him to reel her into his arms, and he sighed into her beautifully silky hair that she'd left loose tonight.

He could, he vowed to himself. He would.

"CAN I TAKE you home?" Beck asked when they'd sat down after several more dances.

Ashni didn't know what to say. 'Yes' seemed obvious. Beck had been walking or driving her home for years. But tonight, she wasn't sure.

Their relationship wasn't working anymore—not for her and maybe not for him. And tonight, after such an emotional day, and the finals and long drive for him, didn't seem like the ideal time to hash it out.

But leaving him hanging didn't seem fair either.

"Yes," she said. "But first let me check in with Sky to make plans for tomorrow."

"Sure," he said and helped her with her cropped denim jacket. He lightly cupped her petal-soft cheek with his work-roughened palm.

"You look beautiful tonight. Even more luminous than usual," he said.

"Thank you," she said, trying to ignore the feelings bombarding her.

"Why does that make you sad?"

A million reasons.

He bent to kiss her, but she slid off the barstool and turned to Sky. Her heart rate shimmered like a hummingbird in her chest.

Beck's naked admiration had always made her feel like she could fly. Now she felt trapped in a cage of her own making.

"I'm going to head out. Beck will walk me back to Walker and Calum's."

Sky nodded. "Have fun."

"No. Not that," she said quickly. "But I do need to talk to him. Try to explain."

Guilt swamped her. She'd confessed more to Sky today than she had to Beck. He was her confidant. And Reeva, who was now married and making a new life. More proof that she needed to create her own new life with work she loved, a home and friends.

"Keep the ball in play," Sky advised. "How about we meet at Main Street Diner at noon, and then review your plan for Harry's House. You can get set up after. I'll help. The kids won't come until three thirty or four."

Ashni nodded. Feeling oddly nervous and anxious, Ashni waved and headed out of Grey's. Beck, tall and determined, paced alongside her.

They needed to talk. She only wished she knew exactly what she wanted to say.

Chapter Five

They walked a block down Main Street—the noise from Grey's fading. This was an impossible situation.

She loved Beck.

She couldn't imagine her life without him.

But she was going to have to. At least until she created a life that didn't revolve around him and wanting him to marry her.

I need to define myself, not be defined by Beck or marriage or children.

She took a deep breath, promptly chickened out and tilted back her head to look at the star-spangled sky.

"I always forget how beautiful the night skies are in Montana."

So many of the places they traveled were cities. She'd grown up in a city. She was tired of the noise and the traffic and the buzz—the never-ending feeling of go-go-go. More. More. More.

"My favorite place to be." His voice rang with conviction.

"And yet you rarely are," she said softly, not meaning it as a criticism but the truth. She'd learned to love Montana with Beck and had always imagined settling down here. Raising their children on the ranch with his granddad, his cousins and their wives and families.

"It never seems like enough time when I'm here," he said.

"Because you don't make it."

His sigh was audible, but Ashni was not feeling forgiving. She'd given him an opening—he could have said Montana was his favorite place to be with her. But he hadn't taken it.

She wanted to kick herself. Why was she still trying?

Force of habit. Habits could be broken.

Ash started walking again.

"Where are we headed?" he asked, and she choked on a laugh that was anything but amused. That was the million-dollar question. Physically, the end of Bramble Lane. Life direction? Love direction? Career direction? Family direction? She hadn't a clue.

This is the new adventure part you're supposed to love.

She wanted to kick her inner sarcasm to the curb along with Beck.

"You want me to drive you? I brought my truck."

In case she invited him to stay. A thrill ran through her. It would be so easy to back away from the ledge she'd climbed on and pretend everything was okay. Let him light her on fire and make her feel loved. Even the touch of his hands and the brushes against her body while they'd been dancing had filled her with heat and longing.

How can I walk away?

She had to. She had to build a life that didn't rely on Beck by her side.

Now that she'd admitted to herself that she wasn't happy, she had to stay true to her course. Create her own happy. Build her new life. Respect and prioritize herself.

It would be hard, but it would get easier.

"I prefer to walk."

"You going to tell me what's wrong?"

No.

Yes.

Ashni stopped in the middle of the sidewalk. "It's hard to put into words," she began, and because it seemed so natural, she reached out, stroking one finger along his much bigger, stronger, work-roughened hand. Even when she knew she needed to get some distance, she still reached for him.

"I don't know where to start."

"Anywhere's good, Ash. Start anywhere. We'll find our way. We always do." He sounded so confident. So sure. And his smile, a little lopsided and wistful, was so familiar and safe that she nearly burrowed into him and just held on.

He felt like part of her, and she didn't know who she'd be without him.

You're about to find out.

Ashni walked toward the courthouse. She always loved the lights on the building at night and the beautiful park that fronted the courthouse and wrapped around it. In a couple of days, tourists would be pouring in for the rodeo. Already most of the shop windows were decorated with rodeo scenes.

It seemed like each year the window dressings became more elaborate even though the friendly competition was more about pride, not prize.

Stop stalling.

"I love you, Beck."

Now there was a news flash to no one ever. Why had she started with that?

He caught her around her waist and pulled her into his body. She thought he'd kiss her, and she felt herself soften.

He lightly cupped her jaw and ran one thumb over her lips.

"I love you too, Ash. You know that. It's always been you."

She searched his eyes, but even with the warm yellow light from the old-fashioned streetlights that were replicas of the town's first gaslights, it was hard to see his expression.

"I know," she said. "But I don't think love is enough anymore."

There was a beat of silence and then another, and another.

"What does that mean?" Beck asked hollowly.

"It's not enough. We want different things from life."

He stared at her—the picture of shock and bewilderment.

"Like what?"

Ashni pulled away from him and continued walking, faster now. How could he be so stupid? *Like what?* Like everything.

But that wasn't fair. Overhearing him ask Bodhi about other women. The clear discomfort when Jerry pressed Beck today about his plans with her. The hurt was raw. But she knew it was more than that. She'd been unhappy for longer. She'd grown more dissatisfied with their life this entire year. She'd felt stuck.

She deserved better. But it was on her to seize it.

"Ash, hold up. Talk to me. Tell me what's really going on." His voice reflected his frustration.

"I don't want to hurt you, Beck, and right now it feels like I'm hurting myself even more, but I want to break up. I need to break up with you."

The words sounded obscene and loud in the night even though she never shouted.

He reared back.

"What are you talking about? Why would we ever break up?"

"Don't tell me you haven't thought about it."

"Never."

"Really? Mister 'I've never ever been with another woman. What's that even like? Do they taste different? Feel different when you're inside them? Is it different when they…you know, blow you? I'll never get the chance to find out.'" She hurled the words at him. Total quote.

She'd even mimicked the wonder in his tone. The curiosity.

His mouth moved but no words came out.

"Like women are different flavors of ice cream for you to

lick and taste. Well, now you've got your chance."

It felt good to raise her voice. Good to be angry. Something inside her felt uncorked—an inner honest emotion genie.

"Go bang other women. Pick them up in bars. Have a competition with never keeps in it his pants, Bodhi. Have at it."

"What?" He still stared at her as if she'd started speaking in tongues. "I don't understand what you're talking about. I'd never cheat. Never."

"Don't play stupid. You asked Bodhi about other women at the sponsor bar in Tucson," she reminded him. "I didn't feel up to going, but then I felt bad about not being there to support you so I showered, got dressed, and arrived to hear you and Bodhi speculating about whether a bunch of buckle bunnies would blow you differently."

Beck squirmed—probably at her crass language, but also because he'd been caught out. Her heart felt like stone, but still the hurt and anger seared her veins. How she wished she'd slapped him at the time—stormed out like a pissed-off diva because this awkward part would have been over then, not just starting. Still, she reveled in the freedom she felt from uncorking the hurt so it fizzed all over him.

"The point is, you wanted to have other experiences with women. Opportunities. Now you have them."

"I don't. I really don't. That was just...talk," he stammered. "Just...you know...dumb guy talk. Bodhi's always with different women. It's so easy for him. I don't understand how he can live like that, and I was just…I don't know…curious. What drives him to pick a different woman every time? I'd had a couple of whiskeys and I just…" He spread out his fingers. "I never acted on it. I wouldn't. I've never even wanted to. I promise, Ash." He looked stricken. "It was just stupid guy talk."

Her fists balled up. Somehow his mumbled sorry excuse left her colder than the glaciers fingering down Copper Mountain. "But that's just the beginning of why I want to break up."

She wanted him to be angry. Push back. Not look as miserable as a dog they'd once seen tossed out a window of a moving truck barreling down a Texas highway. They'd rescued the injured pup and had paid for its treatment at a vet they'd found who'd taken care of it and said he had contacts with a no-kill shelter. Ashni had wanted to keep the shivering mystery mixed-breed dog with the large, sad but hopeful eyes. But it hadn't been "practical with our lifestyle right now"—Beck's words. How she wished she'd ignored him. Two years later she still remembered how it felt to hold the dog, wrapped in her sweater, in her arms while they drove down a rainy highway.

"I don't know what we're doing anymore. Where we're going. We want different things. I'm done following you and your career. I want a dog."

"A…a what? A dog?" Beck repeated. "But you work for the tour. You're head of the…"

"I'm tired of living out of a duffel bag. No future plans

except the next city each weekend. I want to stop living on the road. I want a space to create art. I want to work with kids and families. I want a home. A garden. A kitchen. To sleep in the same bed and yeah, a dog and…"

Your baby.

He jerked like she'd struck him. That told her everything she needed to know. Thank God she'd left the last most precious want in her head.

It was over. Ashni felt cleaved in half. She was probably bleeding out. She felt numb. But she'd started this. She had to be strong and finish it.

"I want to use my science degree. I want to build a career. I want to have a family. You just want to live day to day, racking up points in an endless competition with your cousins."

Beck's eyes sparked and narrowed, and his mouth firmed.

Good.

"I don't fit in that life anymore. I'm tired of trying."

"This is about what Jerry did today at the arena?" Beck demanded, finally on the offense.

Yes! This would be so much easier if he were angry too.

The watery light from the half-moon filtered down through the oak trees in the park and played on the stark planes of his handsome and achingly familiar face.

The demand was a direct hit, but she had far more targets.

"I've felt like this all year," she admitted. "Each year we

talked about you joining up again. We discussed it. This year you signed up without telling me."

He nodded and ran a shaking hand through his thick hair. His other hand white-knuckled his Stetson.

"I did. Bodhi and Bowen were in, so I just automatically re-upped. I should have discussed it with you. I'm sorry."

"Doesn't matter now I'm done. The Jerry thing was just the last nail—or maybe it was that my entire family saw you wiggle out of any sort of commitment to me on national television."

Beck swore.

"Ash, baby." He took a step toward her, and she took two quick steps back. She'd be done if he touched her. Done. She was angry and scared out of her mind at the same time, and she couldn't believe she was going through with this. She craved an exit ramp, and yet at the same time she knew she needed to keep barreling down this road.

He jerked to stand still. It was one of the few times she'd seen him physically awkward. She loved the way he moved—like water or a breeze, so graceful and fluid and certain.

"I'm sorry about today with Jerry. He put me on the spot, and I don't like to talk about us, our private life together."

Of course he'd seize on that excuse.

"It just showed what I've spent too long ignoring. We want different things from life. I want to be happy, and I want you to be happy. So this is the end of the line for us."

"How can I be happy without you?" he demanded. "I

love you."

They were back to the beginning.

"Love isn't enough anymore. I'm bored with the travel. I hate living in the quarters of your rig and the occasional hotel room. I can do my job in my sleep. I want more. I need more. I wish I'd never left that dog behind in Texas," she blurted. "I can't go one more day without making this change."

It was over. She'd killed their relationship. Thirteen, almost fourteen years down the drain.

She stared at him wanting…what? A magic wand? A rewind button? Beck had nodded with each thing she'd said, jaw clenched and tapping his Stetson nervously against his thigh in time with her words.

"This is the end." The words she forced out were a husky whisper.

"You can't just decide that after our whole lives together." He glared at her, swiping his hat through the air. "You can't tell me how I feel or what I need. I love you. I can't imagine my life without you in it, nor do I want to, so clearly I don't need more or some other woman."

The last word sounded like a curse, and Ashni was a bit shocked that she was happy he was so riled. She'd imagined this all so differently. Her crying. Beck solemn. Agreeing with her. Hugging her goodbye and striding off back to the bar, back to his cousins, back to the rodeo.

"Get creative. You'll figure it out. You got a head start with that pink drink blonde."

The sound he made was fascinating—sort of a huff and a growl she'd never heard before. "You know that was nothing. I was trying to be polite."

Ashni didn't respond.

"Why are you dumping all of this on me now?"

Ashni didn't have an answer for that.

"If you've been so bored and unhappy, why not tell me? Why keep me up most of the night getting creative with chocolate the night before leaving for Reeva's wedding if you were so bored and unhappy with me and our lives?"

Her heart practically charged out of her chest, and she could feel her whole body flush. The sudden comprehension in his eyes was unnerving. And wrong. He was totally wrong. He had to be.

"This is about Reeva's wedding."

Dang it.

"All your family jawing on you about us not being married already."

"No," Ashni said, denial choking her. "That did happen," she admitted, resentment burbling up. "You missing such an important family occasion—again—definitely kicked up the gossip to a deafening decibel."

"Ash, baby, I'm sorry. I wanted to go, but I…"

"Needed the points," she finished, refinding her will to see this breakup through. "That's your priority. It's always been your priority. Not me. Not building a life together."

He looked like she'd struck him. "For now," he said in a tight voice, "but—"

"No but. No promises about the future, Beck. You should be free to live your life the way you want. And so should I. I…I love you," she admitted.

"Present tense," he seized the opening. "So why the hell would we break up?"

She sucked in a deep breath and forced her body to settle, to stand still on the sidewalk when she wanted to run and keep running. She'd initially thought that the breakup might be temporary. Something he'd talk her out of by professing undying love, proposing, promising to quit the tour after the finals—seeing their future her way.

Dumb.

And selfish.

"Love is not enough anymore." If she kept saying it, he'd agree, right? "I need move on and be responsible for my happiness."

"And getting married will magically make you happy?" he demanded. "You think marriage will suddenly validate our love and commitment?"

His voice rang out—angry, frustrated. His eyes glittered like topaz jewels embedded in rock. She'd never seen his jaw so clenched, his body so tense.

"Marriage isn't everything," he gritted out. "It doesn't mean a damn thing. It's a piece of paper. It doesn't prove anything. Doesn't keep men from cheating. Or hitting. Or make them take care of their family. Marriage is a tax deduction. A manipulation. A mirage to prove something to somebody else. It doesn't prove what's in my heart, and you,

Ash, you—" he banged hard on his chest "—you are in my heart deep and forever. Seared there sure as a brand on my granddad's cattle. I don't need a marriage certificate to prove my feelings for you. And you shouldn't need that either."

He was angry. So angry. Ash stared, fascinated. He had strung together more words than she could remember at any time. Beck wasn't broody like Bowen, but it was Bodhi who would hold court and entertain her, debating and dissecting any topic with her. Beck listened and joined in. This, this emotional and eloquent man was a fascinating stranger.

"My mom was married four times. Four. That's insane. My dad twice. He ditched two wives and two sets of kids. Walked away. Never looked back. Marriage is no guarantee of anything, especially happiness. Marriage is meaningless."

"Not to me."

She faced him squarely, strangely calm and yet exhilarated. This was it. The first step into her new life.

"You want to get married." His voice was flat. His expression unreadable.

He made marriage to her sound like a really unpleasant chore—like picking up three weeks of dog poop in the backyard in the middle of July.

She laughed. Free. Finally.

"That's just it, Beck. I don't. Not to you. Not anymore."

THE NEXT MORNING, pre-dawn, Beck had fed the ranch

horses, mucked out the stalls, and groomed both Raider and Gallatin. He'd even taken care of Bowen and Bodhi's horses as Bowen had come home late, and Beck wasn't sure Bodhi had come home at all.

Still he wasn't soothed, nor had he found his center. He hadn't slept much last night after Ashni's breakup bomb. It still didn't seem real. A Taylor Swift song came to mind. Had he really missed her signs? Why hadn't she told him she was unhappy instead of just announcing the breakup like that was the only path forward? He was still scrambling to understand.

He'd walked her to her apartment and stood stupidly holding her hands, staring into her beloved face and repeating that he loved her—his only argument. Her reply? A shakily breathed "Beck, stop," and a door closed in his face.

That had hurt. And pissed him off. He'd been unable to sleep, trying to figure out answers to questions he didn't want to ask.

And what was he supposed to do? Give her time? Space? Or fight for her?

Dumb question.

Fight.

No way in hell was he going to indulge what had been a stupid, nosy question to his cousin and chase after some random woman this week.

His empty thermos drove him back to the house. He had to figure out a plan to win back Ash, convince her he was still her man. And for the first time in his life, he couldn't go to his cousins or granddad for help.

He brewed more coffee, staring at the dark liquid steaming and spitting into the pot as if it held the answers he needed. Dammit. He couldn't think. He felt scooped out. Ash was his life. Essential. He felt utterly alone, different without her. And if she kept the door shut, he'd have nowhere to go.

Bodhi would laugh in his face. Clap him on the back and say something pithy like 'game on.'

A rodeo bride.

Ash should be his rodeo bride.

For real. He just had to ask. His public dodge had hurt her. Going to Reeva's wedding alone had hurt her. Last night she'd said she wanted a home and a family.

And a dog.

Hope stirred in his heart. Since they'd graduated college marriage had been hinted at and then, after a couple of years, stated destination everyone steered them toward. It's not that he didn't want to spend the rest of his life with her. He did. But he didn't want his mom's tumultuous relationships and divorce after divorce for him or Ash. The anger. Disappointment. Bitterness. Hate.

I could never hate Ash.

And they were different from his mom and his various stepdads. It was the people who married who screwed it up, not the marriage, right? Marriage wasn't some magical boogeyman that banged on the door with a wrecking ball.

He didn't feel as confident as he should. If he married

Ash, they would still be them, not suddenly transformed into people who no longer talked, laughed, shared, loved.

Like what's happened.

Beck felt sick. Couldn't breathe right. He'd lost her through his inaction. So how did he fight for her? A proposal. He could do that.

But walk away from the rodeo? How could he walk when his cousins needed him the most? Bodhi had become increasingly reckless this year—slipping the leash of his control. Bowen grew more remote each day. Beck felt that he provided balance. And Ash brought the light. The joy that lit them all.

He stared blindly out the kitchen window. No answers except he knew he didn't want to imagine his life without Ash in it.

"Look at you, up and about and on your second thermos," Bodhi greeted him. "That's what a night of make-up sex will do for a cowboy. It's a thing of beauty. Ring shopping today?"

The flash of anger startled him.

"I didn't know you got in." He sucked in a breath, swallowed his reaction.

"Just did."

"I don't want to hear about it, any of it."

"Okay, so no make-up sex." Bodhi looked more interested.

Bowen joined them. "Thanks for getting coffee started."

He looked as ill rested as Bodhi. Apparently, Beck had

been the only one to sleep in his bed last night, alone, although there'd been no sleep to make the early night worth it.

Bowen reached for a mug from the open shelves above the coffee station that had a commercial-sized coffeepot along with a Keurig Ash had bought for their grandfather last Christmas.

Beck had redone the kitchen cabinets on his last break—stripping, sanding, repainting, and rebuilding a few with glass inset doors, and a couple of sets of open shelves. Beck hadn't yet floated the idea of refinishing the floors, but with the moms coming, that probably wouldn't work this time.

But would there be another time?

"Don't engage with Beck. He's cranky. Ash kicked him out of bed."

"You really ought to write fiction." Beck tried to ignore the ribbing. "Or better yet, romance."

"Maybe I will." Bodhi drank deeply from his mug. "But I get enough romance in my life." He stretched, and then took another appreciative swallow of his coffee. "Damn, Beck, you do get one thing right consistently. Coffee."

"One and done is not romance," Granddad chimed in.

All three cousins swiveled to stare at their granddad. He usually let them verbally box, and he never commented about their so-called romantic relationships with women.

"The way you carry on, it's like a competition. Like you're going to get a prize for wrangling the most fillies. You're not. More likely a few cases of STDs and a trip to the public health department for a shot in your butt."

Bodhi flushed and jerked to attention from his sprawl against the counter.

"You're a good man, Bodhi. Find a good woman," he grumped. "And you—" he pointed a tanned, leathery finger at Beck, who winced like he was seven all over again and had messed up one of his chores "—make things right with Ashni. If you think the grass is greener—" he glared at Bodhi and Beck "—one look at Bodhi's absurd antics will spell it out for even the most illiterate cowboy. It's not."

"No, sir," Beck and Bodhi said reflexively.

Granddad pushed the button on the Keurig. "Got a list of chores for you boys in the North Vista barn up on Plum Hill to get it ready for the Bash Sunday night. And the girls have some work for you boys at the cabin as well."

"Consider it done," Bowen said quietly, finishing his coffee.

Granddad took his mug of coffee and went to sit on the front porch—where he always started his day. The front door banged louder than usual, and Beck and his cousins stared at each other, clearly uncomfortable. Bodhi still had a flush high on his cheekbones.

"I'm going to bring Ash a chai and a scone or blueberry muffin from the Java Café. I'll catch up with you at the barn in an hour or so," Beck said, breaking the silence.

"An hour? That's all you got?" Bodhi smirked, recovered from their granddad's rare dressing down. "Takes nearly twenty minutes to get to town."

"Works for me," Bowen said. "Take two hours. I'll need at least that."

"Why?" both Beck and Bodhi demanded.

"We got a game on, right? I don't stand on the sidelines." He grabbed his hat and left the kitchen.

"Seriously?" Beck stared at Bowen who jammed on his boots and reached for his keys. It was barely light, and Bowen had a date this early? With Shauna? His mind rebelled against that idea, but who else?

"You know Ballantynes don't go down without swinging." Bodhi stood and reached for his hat.

Bowen paused at the back door, hand on the handle.

"I don't," Beck said suddenly knowing with total clarity what he was going to do. What he had to do. "I'm all in."

"Hey." Bodhi caught his arm, hard. "Ash is off the board."

Beck squirmed. He could feel Bowen's focused attention from across the kitchen.

"You can't play with her."

"I'm not," he denied fiercely. What did his cousin take him for? "Ash dumped me last night so she's in play."

Bodhi rocked back on his heels. Bowen stared.

"She dumped you?"

"Yeah." It took guts to admit it. "Gonna win her back. I'm buying her a ring any cowboy can see across a dance floor. I'm going to propose to her in front of Granddad and the moms," he said feeling reckless. "And we're going to pick out a dog!"

After the finals.

If that wasn't a commitment, he didn't know what was. Beck kicked into his boots, grabbed his keys, and jammed his hat low on his forehead before Bodhi and Bowen even moved.

"Hell, I'll even marry her at the damn Bash. See if you can top that!" Beck pushed open the back door and headed for his truck, his mind made up and his blood burning with determination.

He heard his cousins coming up behind, and he started to run. Their footsteps pounded the dirt fast and familiar behind him, and Beck increased his speed, smiling. It was going to be okay.

"You're on, cowboy," Bodhi called out, just like Beck knew he would.

"Don't count on your Plum Hill until the foundation is poured," Bowen said.

Beck laughed and reached his truck.

"I dare you," he said to both of his cousins. "Double dare."

Their eyes flared. It was all kinds of crazy, but it felt good. Beck got in his truck and started his engine, peeling out ahead of Beck and Bodhi, just a little.

Chapter Six

THERE WAS AN actual line at the Java Café. Each time Beck came back to Marietta, the Java Café seemed busier. Something was new or there was a menu change. Marietta might be small, but it wasn't standing still. The Java was far more than a coffee shop—it served a small, but hearty and delicious breakfast selection and offered a lunch menu for the steady grab-and-go customers who worked the ranches, construction sites, first responders, and local hospital and medical offices.

Sally Driscoll, a barista for as long as he could remember, pulled shots like a pro and kept up a steady stream of conversation while not missing a beat taking customers' orders.

"Hey, Beck, good to see you." Boone Telford, a local whom he'd competed against in the summer rodeos stepped in line behind him. "I saw that you were competing again this year at Copper Mountain—slumming it." Boone laughed. He too had followed the pro rodeo tour for quite a few years but always came home to compete at the Copper Mountain Rodeo.

"Hardly." Beck was happy to see Boone. He was easy-going and had always been quick to help others and generous with his time and volunteering. "Copper Mountain Rodeo feels like home. You riding?"

"Nah, I had my time." He waved his left hand, which had a thick, gold wedding band. "Officially retired. Found a girl at the beach in Cali last spring, brought her home in the summer and got married all in the same year. Piper's the best thing that ever happened to me, but we're due to have something even better in a couple of months. Can't wait. Building a house on the ranch. Working with my dad but got a few side hustles going."

Boone had always been quick with a smile and a deluge of information.

"Wow. Married."

In a year.

Expecting.

Retired.

Boone was his age.

"That's a lot to take in." Beck's mouth felt dry. "Fast."

"Why wait?" His smile split his face. "When you know, you know." His face shadowed. "Oh. Ummmmm. I didn't mean…you still with Ashni, right?"

"Yeah." Beck ignored the hard kick in his gut. They weren't broken up. This was just temporary. Very temporary.

"Great." Boone's shoulders relaxed, and he was all smiles again. "Can't imagine you guys apart. She's been in your cheering section since high school."

She had been. Always cheering him on, which hit him

wrong today.

"Bringing her a chai and some pastries as a Monday morning treat." Beck felt the unusual need to defend himself. "She's teaching an after-school art class at Harry's House this week."

Boone nodded. "Oh, yeah? Must be the one my cousin's taking—a guest cartoonist. Petal's been talking about it all month. The kids got sketchbooks ahead of the class and were told to take pictures of at least ten people doing something and to tell a story about it with dialogue or a thought bubble. Petal's been on a mission. Her book's nearly full. She's excited."

Pride washed through Beck. And then shame. Ashni had so much to offer. So many talents, but she'd been following him in his career now full-time far longer than the one or two years they'd initially discussed.

Beck tried to shrug off this new, uncomfortable feeling. He and Ash would work this out. She was just stirred up from Reeva's wedding. And Jerry's dumb stunt. And his dumber response.

"Hey, you should bring Ashni one night to dinner. You could meet Piper. She's a masseuse in town. She had an early client this morning so I'm bringing something for her break then heading back to work on the house. If you and Ashni come by for dinner, I can show you around. I'm setting up a rodeo school for kids—an after-school program in conjunction with Harry's House. Got some retired cowboys helping out. Kane Wilder's helping with financing. We're working with little kids and then we'll have more of a development program out on the ranch for older kids, who are more serious. Something to think about when your time comes. Your turn to order."

Feeling a little like he'd been knocked off a bucking bronc and kicked for his trouble, Beck ordered the chai extra hot, hoping to keep it as warm as possible, and his drip coffee, and then exchanged cell numbers with a still-smiling Boone, who was greeting nearly everyone in the place.

An unexpected rush of longing hit him.

Beck knew many people in town, but not like Boone, who'd grown up ranch. He hadn't had to split his time between his beloved ranch and city life with such different expectations.

City boys. Summer cowboys. Country hicks.

Shaking off the half-remembered taunts from both sides, Beck walked the few blocks to Bramble Lane, hoping to clear his head. Boone—his happiness, his certainty, his plans— still echoed in his brain.

He mounted the outside stairs of the carriage house over a four-car garage and knocked on the door.

"It's open." Ash's voice floated through an open window.

It felt strange to feel nervous. Ash was his life, part of him. And yet last night she'd closed the door on him. Told him they were through.

And today he was going to change her mind.

The studio apartment appeared to be spacious—full of light—wide windows, a few skylights in the peaked ceiling that was composed of whitewashed tongue-in-groove wide planks—similar to the floor. A full kitchen with a white quartz island with four barstools. And a comfortable seating area.

Not sure where to put the coffee down, in the kitchen or in the sitting area with the white plush furniture and colorful pillows and throws, he prowled. And then stopped, seeing the large, plush, artistic horse sitting upright in a chair—the goofy expression on its face, the rakish beret and paintbrush in its mouth, and the palette on an extended hoof.

"Did you forget something?" Ash came out of the bathroom, dark hair gleaming. "Oh." She paused and pressed her lips together. A flush stole across her cheeks, and she didn't meet his searching gaze. He could see her pulse hammer in her delicate neck. "Beck."

"Where'd you get this?" he asked, feeling stupid.

She was still buttoning up her denim shirt dress, and he couldn't help that his gaze narrowed on her slim fingers on the buttons, closing off the tantalizing view of her satiny skin.

"Bodhi."

"Bodhi?"

Ash jolted and frowned. "Why are you yelling?"

What was Bodhi doing at Ash's apartment? He'd said nothing about winning the horse. Nothing about stopping off this morning. And how had Bodhi known where Ash was? A suspicion gnawed at his brain and twisted his gut, but it was too…too impossible.

"What is wrong with you?"

He stared at her in disbelief. How could she ask that when she'd dumped him last night with no warning?

"He just dropped it off a few minutes ago for you," Ashni said. "What's the big deal?"

He moved his mouth, brain trying to keep up, but nothing, not a word emerged.

"He said you won it for me yesterday." She crossed her arms. "But clearly he was once again helping you out." Her beautiful mouth pursed, and her eyes sparked.

"I did." He sat down, feeling like his legs couldn't quite hold him up. What had he been thinking—that somehow Bodhi was making a move on Ash? It was ludicrous. Bodhi was a player, but he was loyal. "Before the finals I saw it and thought of you." He paused and looked at her, willing her to come closer. Sit down with him. "I won it with help from Bodhi and Bowen," he admitted in full confession mode.

"But when we were walking back to get ready for the finals, we saw a little girl with her mom. Without a dad. She had a…a…port." He touched near his collarbone. "And she was holding the coloring book you made. She recognized me on the cover."

Ash closed her eyes, looking pained.

"I gave the horse to her and tickets in the VIP sections since you weren't coming in until later."

Only she'd never come.

"I'm glad," Ash said.

"I missed you, Ash. I wanted to have a present for when I

picked you up so I went back after my events, but the second grand prize had already been won—by Bodhi or both of them."

It would be like his cousins to have his back but to not make a big deal about it, not even telling him. "I wanted it for you." He took a sip of his coffee. God, his hand shook. "I suppose you think that's stupid."

"No. Sweet."

His heart soared, but she didn't move from her position against the doorjamb of what he assumed led to the bathroom. Ash always told him he was sweet, and Bodhi never missed an opportunity to mock him. But sweet didn't seem enough today. Ash looked unimpressed and unrelenting.

"Will you sit with me a spell? I brought you a chai and…"

"Beck." She sighed. "We broke up. I don't want to hurt you. Or drag out this hard part. But you need to stop coming around."

"I don't want to."

"I do."

He didn't know what to say to that. He'd come here to fight for her. To charm her. To do something to make this right, to make this awful feeling go away, but he'd really been hoping that she would have changed her mind, realized her mistake, welcomed him back into her arms, and being a stupid dumbass, he'd hoped to be back in her bed.

"This isn't easy for me either." She made an impatient sound as she swept her chai off the coffee table and resumed standing in the doorway.

"Then why do it?"

"I have to."

"Why?"

"I need to do something different."

"Then do it. Anything. Just do it with me. Let me be a part of your life."

He sounded pathetic. He felt worse. And it wasn't working. At. All. But Beck had never played any games with Ashni. He hadn't had to win her. She'd just always been his. He hadn't ever had to try. They just worked.

And now they didn't.

She stared down at her chai. "I don't want to continue as we were because then I won't make any changes, and I need to. I'm not happy, and it's not your fault. It's mine. I've drifted, and I need to stop. I need to make a life for myself that has challenge and meaning. I need to try something new, and I can't do that while still trotting after you city to city doing the same job. And you need to pursue your dreams without guilt or worrying about my happiness."

"Your happiness is my happiness," he mumbled more miserable than he'd been last night. How was that even possible?

She took a quick gulp of the chai and then made a face.

"What is this?"

"Chai. The spicy kind with two percent milk. Just like you like." He jumped up. It had better be chai.

"Tastes weird." She made a face, sticking out her tongue,

just like the yuck emoji.

Beck checked the cup. It was marked properly. He tasted it.

"Yeah. Chai. Tastes like it always does."

"No, it doesn't." She took the cup back and walked over to the sink. "It tastes off, but thank you for thinking of me, for bringing me a chai."

He felt so awkward, like nothing in his body was working properly. Everything hurt.

Even looking at her. She was so beautiful but far away. Nervously, he looked around the room, knowing he should leave, but afraid that if he did, he'd never see her again. His eyes lit on her guitar. The one he'd made for her in wood shop and with the help of a guitar maker in Denver. It was out of the case, so she'd been playing it last night or this morning.

That was something. She wasn't throwing everything of them away.

"I love you," he said, knowing he was going to walk out the door. "I always have. I know I always will. We've been through a lot together. Grown up together."

Tears gathered in her eyes, and even though he hated to make her cry, it was at least a sign that she felt something, and he had to grab on to that. Make a plan. Run with it. But he needed to give her some time alone, just not as much as she thought she wanted. Definitely not forever.

"I'm not ready to give up on us, Ash, but I do want you to be happy."

With me.

"You're not responsible for my happiness, Beck."

Everything inside of him shouted to get out of here, regroup. But he wasn't used to quitting. He thought of argument after argument, but discarded them all, then something Bodhi had said to him that stupid, fateful night that had so riled Ash rose up in his mind.

"Walk away before you're ready. Makes 'em hungry for more."

Is that what Ash was doing? A game to get him to propose? Quit the tour?

It was anathema to their entire relationship. She had never been manipulative. The games he, Bodhi and Bowen engaged in made her roll her eyes or laugh. But…wasn't that what he was doing to her?

Guilt edged into his pain. Game playing between lovers wasn't right, was it? But if she were playing a game with him, that meant she hadn't given up on them.

Hope soared.

So what exactly was his next play?

For the first time since yesterday, he felt a spark of hope and…intrigue.

He walked over to her, keeping his limbs loose. She'd always loved the way he walked. He'd never really understood that. He just walked, but sometimes after a competition when he'd walk toward her, she'd run toward him, jump into his arms and kiss him like she'd never let him go. He'd feel the heat of her desire roll off of her.

This time she pressed back against the kitchen sink, her eyes flared, and he saw the pulse in her neck kick up.

He stopped close enough to touch her, but he didn't.

"Your happiness is my happiness." He repeated the phrase, meaning it. "Take the time you need, Ash." He waited a beat. To kiss or not? A brush of his lips or…let her think he'd kiss her?

"Beck," she whispered. "You can't."

He leaned down, his mouth close to her ear so that his breath ruffled her hair.

"I can. I want to, but I won't."

And then he did the hardest thing he'd ever done.

He walked away.

⭐

BECK WALKED BACK to his truck, his mind raced unable to focus on anything. Once, a few years ago, a bucking bronc had thrown and kicked him, slamming him into the arena's metal fencing resulting in a concussion, despite his helmet. The bronc had hopped up, pissed, and strutted away, lunging at the rodeo clowns a few times before heading back to the chute as if it had been his plan the entire time. First and only time he'd been carried out of an arena on a stretcher. He'd come to a groggy sort of awareness in an ambulance with a tearful Ashni holding his hand and pressing ice to the massive lump that had been developing slightly above his temple.

He felt the same now.

Only worse.

And he needed to be on top of his game. Not at the bottom.

Ashni wanted space. He needed to give her some but not too much.

Blowing out a breath, he unlocked his truck with the remote and climbed in. Slammed the door as if that would hold in the emotions roiling around inside of him.

Space was the last thing he wanted to give her. The urge to return to her apartment and lock the door until they hashed things out spooked him. He wasn't like that at all. Bossy. Controlling. They had a partnership.

Or so he'd thought.

While he had thought he and Ash were happy, she'd been slowly growing apart from him. It was like that Taylor Swift song Ashni had loved so much she'd played it over and over on her guitar the past few months while they'd been driving.

What was it called? "Exile." Great. The title might as well have been a billboard that she'd slammed over his head.

Beck sat in his truck, not sure he could drive. His breath shuddered in and out. He hated this—feeling helpless, out of control. He squeezed his eyes shut, trying to calm his racing heart and mind.

Ashni had made it sound like she'd been unhappy for some time and he'd been some unfeeling, selfish jerk. And then to imply that her happiness was hers alone to find—like he had no part. He was calling BS on that. He wanted her happy. He wanted her fulfilled. She could have that and more with him. But she had to let him in on what she needed and what was missing. He wasn't some sideshow psychic with a tarot deck and crystal ball.

He started up his truck and drove. He watched while several families crossed the street near the Java Café. An idea occurred to him. Ashni's art class started this afternoon. Kids liked food. They'd be hungry after school. He could at least do that. Order some food for later in the day and deliver it himself—visit the classroom, meet the kids, see Ashni in the new life she wanted to create.

Be supportive but casual. He was good with kids. He'd interact with the kids for a couple of minutes and then leave before Ashni could wonder at his motives.

He shifted into drive, squinting through the windshield. Was the sun always so bright? The sky so blue? He felt like he'd just been thrust into a world where everything was too bright. Too vivid. The air shimmered with heat. It was like he was seeing everything for the first time—different, but the same, only more glaring.

It took him a moment to realize he'd been so thrown by his conversation with Ash that he'd left his hat behind. Better than leaving without his boots or pants. That had happened to Bodhi once. Best call for help Beck had ever received. They'd been in college and, for once, Bodhi's Prince Charming crown had been just a bit tarnished.

As if thinking of his cousin conjured him up, he saw Bodhi enter the Java Café and take a seat in the window with the same woman he'd been talking to and dancing with at Grey's last night. Nico somebody. They spoke animatedly. Bodhi spotted him through the window, smirked, and gave him a thumbs-up. Then Beck received a text.

"Game on?"

"Definitely."

He just needed a strategy. And the four people he relied on most as his north stars were all on opposing sides.

The road was now clear so Beck continued slowly down Main Street. He'd call in the order to the café—seeing Bodhi in full suitor mode didn't sit well. Work would clear his head so he could formulate a plan of attack.

"Supposed to be love, not war," he murmured.

As he drove by the Graff Hotel, he saw Bowen exiting down the wide curved staircase of the entrance, walking hand in hand with a woman with short platinum hair.

She looked a bit familiar.

But it was the handholding that shocked him. His cousin had pulled into town near sundown last night, and just past sunup, he'd raced all of them into town and now he was coming out of a hotel with a woman and heading toward the Main Street Diner. It wasn't Shauna from last night. She was likely nursing a hangover from deeper than one of the seven pits of hell.

"Hey," Beck slowed down and shouted out the window. Had even Bowen lost his mind?

Bowen looked both ways and jogged to the truck, still

holding the woman's hand. She was much smaller than Bowen and had huge, amber colored eyes that reminded him of whiskey. Her smile was impish.

"What are you doing?" Beck asked, stupidly—as if he didn't know, but seeing Bowen faux wooing turned his stomach. Usually their challenges pitted their strengths, skills and wits against each other—no one else was involved so no one could get hurt.

"Remember Langston? Best barrel racer on the Montana teen circuit back in the day?"

"Hey, Beck. Good to see you. Bowen's doing a huge favor for me this week." She stood on tiptoes and kissed Bowen's jaw. "For practice."

Her smile looked like the sun. Bowen stared into her heart-shaped face like he was under a spell. What was going on? Bowen needed a favor. What did Lang need?

"Earth to Bowen," Beck muttered.

"Looks like we're running the board." Bowen grinned at him and knocked twice on the truck. "See you back at the ranch."

Sliding his arm around her slim waist, Bowen walked them back to the sidewalk and toward the diner. It wasn't until Beck heard the light toot of a horn behind him that he realized he was just sitting there, idling in the middle of Main Street.

With Bodhi taking the same woman out twice in a row and Bowen publicly holding hands, the Rodeo Bride Game was most definitely on.

"Dummmm. Dum. Dum. Dummmm." He hummed the wedding march or something like it under his breath.

It was a dumb game. Someone was going to get hurt. But Granddad's future was on the line. Hell, all of their futures were on the line, and he was all in.

ASHNI SAT ON the floor with the twelve students who'd signed up to take the mural class. She'd expected mostly girls, but perhaps the cartooning description had sounded more graphic like video games or anime, so an equal number of boys had signed up.

For the first half hour of class, they'd played an introduction game by doing a quick sketch illustrating a memory of something they had done or an accomplishment, and kids guessed the meaning. The ice breaker had been a hit. The students were engaged, and the energy and creative buzz was heady.

But she'd yet to approach the idea of building their individual story panels into a cohesive theme for the mural, which would be critical. That was her goal before they ended class today.

The only problem—Ashni was suddenly hungry. She'd been too keyed up to eat after her conversation with Beck this morning.

Stop thinking of him.

She refocused on the group and then encouraged them to

brainstorm themes for their mural panels.

"Rodeo," one pre-teen boy called out.

Beck flashed through her mind again—his smile, his swagger when he'd walk toward her, arm out, palm up, fingers beckoning, the wicked heat in his eyes…

Stop!

She was stronger than this. Beck was a habit she could break. She typed *rodeo* onto her tablet, and it showed up on the large interactive whiteboard behind her.

"The history of Marietta," another kid called out.

"That's like school. Boring," William, the kid with the rodeo suggestion, dismissed.

"Gunfights. Blood and guts, hookers at Grey's," a kid named Jacob countered, and she wondered if she should object to his language.

"That would be all right then, like a video game," William admitted. They fist-bumped and made exploding noises.

"We want ideas. And discussion. Not judgment. Please don't shut anything or anyone down. We want a large list." Ashni ignored the blood and guts and hookers themes. "As an artist you need your mind to be open to bounce around a lot of ideas before settling on one you want to explore. Then the real play and fun begins." She smiled at her students. "You need an open mind and to be kind or else the creativity—yours and others'—will get shut down."

It would have been a great moment—maybe—except her stomach—iffy for the past few weeks—chose that moment to interject. Loudly.

"Oops!" She had to laugh at their surprised expressions. "Excuse me."

She'd meant to buy snacks for her students. She'd discussed it with Sky over the lunch she had picked at but not eaten, but then she'd been too busy setting up the room, changing and rechanging her mind and making plans with Sky to come out and see her studio the next day.

"Tomorrow I'll bring snacks," she promised.

"How about some snacks today?" a way too familiar deep drawl of a voice interrupted.

Beck.

And her stupid heart hopped and jigged.

He entered the classroom, wearing a different Stetson because his was still on her couch, judging her until she had picked it up and put it in the coat closet on the top shelf. Beck's black tee stretched tight over his sculpted torso, Wranglers faded and worn hugged his hips and thighs in a way she should not be noticing in a room full of children.

Please don't let him turn around.

Beck's prime ass had been her undoing countless times. Even after all these years together, his backside still struck her stupid. And when he was walking…Ashni felt a wave of heat wash over her. Humiliating, because she'd told him they were breaking up and she didn't want to be sending mixed messages, but her body wasn't mixed up at all. It wanted Beck. Badly.

If she could kick herself, she would. *Stupid body.*

The kids goggled at him, then peppered him with questions.

"Beck." She had to take charge of the situation. She was the teacher. It would be easier if her heart would stop fluttering in her throat so she could breathe and speak properly.

"You shouldn't…you…" She wasn't quite sure what to say. What about break up did he not get? She'd been clear this morning. Adamant.

"Stalker" was not what she'd been intending to mutter under her breath while he grinned.

"C'mon now," he said. "You know I can't stay away."

He could learn.

But she was standing too close and staring at him like he was some kind of superhero who'd just swooped in to save the day in a Hollywood blockbuster.

"Yeah, rodeo cowboys." One of the older girls nudged one of her friends. "That should so be our theme."

"Where should I put the food?" Beck asked, looking around the room.

Half the group jumped to their feet.

"Hey now, settle," Beck said, and with no more than a nod of his head, the boys and several girls sank back down on the floor. "Your teacher will tell when it's break time. I was trying to sneak in the back—" he smiled like a sunrise "—but picked the wrong door."

Like Beck could sneak into any room in the world unnoticed.

Swimming against the tide.

No. She'd been letting herself get sucked into Beck's orbit for far too long.

"Thank you," she said, sounding so prim she wanted to kick her own darn behind. "Please set the food on that table over there. Do you need some…um…?" She broke off not wanting to walk into any flirty games with Beck.

Too late.

His eyes crinkled with warmth and gleamed.

"Help? Desperately," he whispered the last word at her as he put down the massive plate of sandwiches. He also carried two bags—one from Monroe's grocery store, which contained apples and oranges. The other bag was from the bakery.

"Beck." She wanted to be stern, but the gesture was so sweet, so Beck, that for a moment she was afraid her willpower would sputter out.

"You're welcome." He leaned toward her. He was going to kiss her. Her eyes fluttered shut, but then she remembered.

Kids.

They'd broken up.

"Is that your boyfriend?" one girl asked.

"No."

"Yes."

They spoke at the same time.

"Ooooooh." A multitude of voices shared their thoughts on the contradiction.

"I call yes," one girl named Meghan said.

"Definitely," another girl sighed.

"Hey, if we do a rodeo theme, we'd need a model," Meghan sounded like she was thirteen going on thirty. "All sketch classes have models pose."

Beck smiled. "Wouldn't be my first time." He grinned at the group, and Ashni wanted to kick him in his prime behind. Why were her thoughts so violent? Beck looking gorgeous and posing was not in her curriculum.

"Naked," Meghan's friend Crystal said matter-of-factly.

Beck's smile faded. Ashni laughed.

"Time to go. We're keeping this class G-rated." She motioned Beck toward the door. "Thank you very much, Mr. Ballantyne, for the snacks."

The confusion on Beck's face along with the kids' ping-ponging gazes was pretty funny. No one knew where to look—the longed-for food so temptingly displayed on the table, Beck, or her.

What story would this scene tell?

Of course, Ashni had no intention of asking the kids that question because she didn't want to know. But their next exercise was to come up with abstract feelings—happiness, anger, excitement—and figure out how to represent them with images.

After their snack.

But she wouldn't admit that to Beck because she didn't want to give him an excuse to linger.

"Ma'am." Beck winked and tipped his hat. "Muralists."

He tipped his hat to them. "Can I steal your teacher for a moment?"

Oh. No.

"Ooooooooooh," the Greek chorus of doom sang out again.

Not wanting to make a fuss, Ashni smiled and walked Beck toward the door with a confidence she didn't feel.

She pulled him out into the hall so she could still see her group in the small art room, but they couldn't overhear the conversation.

"Beck, thank you for the snacks. It was very thoughtful," she said quickly, "but I meant what I said this morning."

"I know you did, Ash."

"So, you need to stop coming by."

Why was this getting harder, not easier? And why was he nodding?

"I will," he said. "I just feel like I don't really understand, and I want to. You really sprung this on me. I know you've likely been thinking about it for months."

Guilt coursed through her. She hadn't. Not like this. Breaking up. Had she? She'd been unhappy traveling. She'd felt at loose ends. Professionally unfulfilled. But Beck…Confusion clouded her judgment. She didn't know how to explain it to him. Or she did, and he wasn't listening.

"I just feel like I need a little…closure. And maybe if I could take you to dinner and we could talk, I could say what I need to say so that I too can move on."

Move on? She blinked. He was moving on? One dinner

and chat, and he'd be ready to move on—after half their lives together?

Isn't that what you want?

"I want you to enjoy your week of teaching. I know you're going to do great. You're fantastic at everything you do, Ash, and I mean that."

Her rush of happiness was visceral. "Thank you." His opinion still meant so much to her.

"And I've got a lot of work to do at the ranch this week, and the moms are coming in and the rodeo will be starting, so I'll be out of your hair, but I need to be able to concentrate so if we could talk tonight over dinner it might help me to get in a better headspace."

He paused, and his voice lowered. "I'm worried about Granddad."

"What? Why?" Alarm skittered through her. "He seemed fine when we made dinner yesterday." But he'd acted strange when she'd mentioned she'd be staying in town because of the class. He'd seemed…she wasn't really sure. Almost like he'd been expecting something.

He'd actually looked at her like Beck was now—like he was trying to see into her soul.

"I think he's worried. Covering something up. I was going to talk to you about it, run a couple of ideas by you, but now…"

"You can tell me anything," she said quickly, and then she nearly groaned.

He couldn't. They were broken up. By her request. But she felt like Ben Ballantyne was her granddad too. And she had a room full of kids who were definitely getting restless.

"Fine. Dinner," she said hastily, already regretting it.

"I'll pick you up at seven."

"No, I'll meet you," she insisted. She needed control and a sense of separation.

Beck didn't like that. He was too much of an old-school cowboy, and for a moment, she nearly smiled. Even when they'd been kids, he'd insisted on walking her home, carrying her backpack, even though she lived in the opposite direction.

"Rosita's?" he asked.

She nodded and turned away before he could do something to further weaken her resolve. It was ridiculous how all he had to do was show up, and she felt gooey inside. She needed to remember him speculating about some other woman imitating a vacuum cleaner. Or squirming under Jerry's questions.

Her phone buzzed with a message. Crawford County Health Department. Her heart nearly jumped in her chest. That was fast. Good news or bad? She had to resist the urge to check the voice message. She'd do it during the break. She looked behind her, one hand on the doorjamb to the art room, feeling like she was straddling two worlds.

Beck walked away. The kids in the classroom and the message regarding her impulsive job application waited on the other side.

Ashni walked back inside her classroom and kicked the door shut with her foot.

Chapter Seven

Beck dipped a tortilla chip into the fresh, house-made salsa and crunched down. He'd been to hundreds of Mexican restaurants during his travels. Rosita's was in his top three—maybe number one because it was local, like he was. Almost. But that feeling of belonging, just like the hazy view of his future, felt like a puff of smoke dissipating in the night sky.

Nothing felt right anymore.

He'd thought hard about his approach with Ash all day as he and his cousins had repaired part of the barn roof and some loose slats, but no plan had emerged except trying to understand what really was the problem so he could fix it. He, Bodhi and Bowen had worked mostly in silence. Bodhi and Bowen hadn't mentioned their evening escapades or breakfast dates. Their rhythm was off to the extent that Bowen had even missed a nail and hit the knuckle of his thumb while he'd been up on the roof. It had been his hold hand, and although rodeo cowboys and ranch hands got injured a lot, it just seemed like one more foreboding messenger of disaster.

Beck kept watching the door and trying to not check his

watch. His stomach churned, anticipating Ashni. She'd been his other half since high school. And now he was nervous and worried about making things worse.

"You ready for that margarita yet, cowboy? It might stop that leg you keep bouncin' from spilling any more chips," the server casually flirted. "First date?"

She scanned the outside sidewalk the way he'd been doing for the past ten minutes. Ashni was never late. Never. Her punctuality was only one of the many traits he admired about her.

"Feels like." He couldn't dredge up a smile.

"I'm sure she'll come unless she's stupid."

"Definitely not stupid."

And maybe that was the problem.

Maybe he did need to play this more—like this morning when he'd leaned close like he was going to kiss her, but he didn't, or this afternoon when he hinted about Granddad and walked away. But playing with Ashni felt all sorts of wrong. And yet he'd tossed his hat into the Rodeo Bride Game, betting he'd really marry her.

Maybe if he gave her space it would reinforce that she was making the wrong decision. Or what if she realized it was the right one?

His stomach flopped nauseatingly. No. She wouldn't walk away from thirteen years together. She was feeling neglected. She'd want him to give chase. He needed to keep thinking of this as a game—with astronomically high stakes.

"So…" The server's husky voice brought him back to

reality. "How 'bout I bring you a margarita while you wait for your friend. And if she doesn't show, I have a break coming. I could join you."

"Thank you. Yes, to the margarita, but I'm expecting my girl. We had a bit of a…" How to define what was going on in a handful of words? He helplessly gestured, and her face creased in sympathy.

"I hope you work it out," she said kindly. "Shall I bring two margaritas then?"

Normally, he would say yes. Ash didn't drink much, but she did love a margarita on the rocks with chips and salsa and guacamole. He looked at the fresh guac. He hadn't dipped into it yet to save it for her. It was weird to feel hungry but also sick to his stomach. But since she thought he wasn't attuned to her needs, he should let her order her own drink.

"Just one to start. And check back when she arrives."

If she comes.

And there she was, her blue-black waves tumbling over her shoulders, swinging free like she was in a shampoo commercial and catching the last of the sun's rays as she carefully looked both ways before crossing the street.

She wore a yellow sundress that hugged her small frame, a cropped denim jacket, and a diaphanous multicolored long scarf from one of her *salwar kameezes* was draped gracefully around her neck and flowed down her back. She ran her hand through her hair as she entered the restaurant, and the henna tattoo from the wedding looked so elegant and elaborate drifting over her hands and up over her wrists.

Beck stood. His knees felt weak, his heart pounded.

"Don't let her know she's getting to you."

How was he supposed to do that? He couldn't breathe. She looked so beautiful and elegantly stylish. And he wasn't the only one who noticed. The room quieted. More than a few people stared. Ash caught sight of him, but her eyes didn't light up. She didn't smile.

Usually Beck would walk toward her. Take her hand. Hug her. But he felt rooted to the floor in misery.

I'm losing her.

He could feel it.

"Ash." He managed to squeeze out the syllable. He took her hands in his much larger ones. They were chilled. His shook. He didn't even try to dredge up a smile.

He held the chair for her as Ashni gracefully sat, perching on the edge almost like a bird about to take flight.

How had this misery and strangeness happened? It seemed impossible. He knew her as well as himself. She was part of him, yet tonight she was a stranger.

Hell. I feel like a stranger.

His drink came.

"Margarita?" the server asked.

Ashni hesitated. Looked at his. Worried her bottom lip then shook her head. "No, thank you. Water is fine."

"I got your favorite, guac," he said unnecessarily.

Ash didn't eat. She played with her fork. Moved her water glass around. This was awful.

"How was your class?" Surely, that was a safe topic.

"Good." She stared at her water glass. Still no eye contact. Then she pressed her palms on her thighs. She only did that when she was nervous, bracing herself for something hard or unpleasant.

Calm down.

His mind raced as fast as it had when he'd been in elementary school when sitting still had been dang near impossible and learning even harder.

"The kids. They seemed really excited to be there," he offered desperately.

She nodded.

"How did you enjoy your first day of teaching them?" He better get a lineup of questions to fire at her, anything to get her to talk, to look at him, to tell him what he really needed to know. "Was it what you expected?"

"I was nervous." She touched her fingertips to the water glass and ran her thumb up and down the side. Beck felt a jolt of heat to his chest and then lower as his stupid cock perked, noticing her move because she had often stroked him the same way.

Even her lips—pursed in a frown—looked sensuous and tempting. He shifted in his seat. She wasn't doing it on purpose to tease him by jacking him up. She'd never had to try.

"I'd been anticipating this for a couple of months now."

Beck felt nailed to his chair with guilt. He'd forgotten about the class. Bodhi had had to remind him.

"Thinking of different ways of doing things, researching." Her voice warmed, and her expression lit with enthusiasm.

I've been such a selfish jerk.

He *had* been taking her for granted. Not paying attention to her or her needs. He'd been so caught up in his own worries about his dip in points and earnings, watching Bodhi soar ahead but behave more recklessly. And Bowen had drifted further away every day.

She's talking, moron. Listen.

"I had so many ideas and so many imaginings of how things might work or the disasters that might happen. But it was easier than I thought. I worried I'd blank out or feel self-conscious, but the kids made it easy. Everything flowed, and the plans I made for the first lesson worked."

She finally looked up into his face.

He felt another jolt to his chest from that liquid-black gaze. He covered her small hands that still played up and down on the glass.

"All the kids were engaged, and they'd filled out their journals, and we talked about what Marietta means to them. The kids seem really lit."

"I'm not surprised, Ash. You're good at everything you do. I knew you'd be a spectacular teacher. The kids are lucky to have you."

"Marietta always seemed to be a bit magical." She tilted her head and seemed to look at him more deeply. "The way you always talked about it. As if it's where you are truly happy. Where you belong. Marietta always seemed like where your heart is."

"Ash, you are where my—"

"I feel lucky," she said quickly, interrupting him. "This opportunity…" she paused and moistened her upper lip with the tip of her tongue "…came at a really good time."

He stared, fascinated at her unconscious sexy move then yanked his mind out of the gutter.

"Yeah?" he encouraged even though everything she said made him feel more and more unworthy. He'd been on the brink of telling her that wherever she was, was his home, which was so *not* the way to play it cool.

"I loved planning out the class, and teaching the kids really centers me in the moment. I can't think about anything else, and I feel part of a team—a little bit how the drama productions and band made me feel in high school—part of something bigger than myself, with a common purpose. I've missed that."

Silence between them. Awkward, when it had never been before. Ash had filled the silences with warmth, humor and intelligent observations.

And now it was his turn to build her up.

"Ash, I'm so sorry," he breathed. His wants had pulled her so far away from what *she* wanted.

"Have you decided what you want to eat?"

The server popped in with the worst timing ever.

Tell her you'll quit the tour.

Ask her to marry you.

His inner voice was urgent. And maybe more than a little crazy.

Beck sat back in his chair and watched her jump all in with the interruption, whereas he wanted to send the server away. Heck, he wanted to pick up Ashni and rush her to his truck and just keep driving.

Yeah. That would go over well. So much for being a supportive partner. And it hit him then that this awful part, this aloneness, this cold emptiness was his to fix. He had to breach the gap, not by getting her to change her mind, but by becoming the change she needed.

He stared at Ash as she smiled at the server and quickly scanned the menu. The server pointed at some menu items, but Beck just felt blindsided by his own realization and what it meant.

"I am so stupid."

Both women stared at him.

"Lucky." The server smiled at Ash. "Not all men can admit when they F it up. Something to eat?" she asked him.

"Tacos."

Because tacos made everything better. Except this.

And tacos wouldn't get him out of the hole he'd dug. He felt ripped in half. He wanted to give her the time and space to build the life she wanted, but he also wanted to hold on to her. Trust that his love for her and hers for him would be enough to keep their marriage strong so it wouldn't be a revolving door like his mom's marriages. Maybe he should propose. But he could hardly pop the question over a basket of chips after more than thirteen years and no sparkling ring that would demonstrate the depth of his love. Her specialness and how crucial she was to his next breath.

So what was his plan? Give her the space she claimed she wanted or propose now?

Marriage was what she wanted last Christmas, but now he was contemplating a proposal in an unromantic Mexican restaurant without a ring while his cousins played a Rodeo Bride Game—which he could win if he proposed.

Or get a basket of chips thrown at him.

The server and Ash stared at him.

"What?" What had he missed after announcing he was stupid and tacos? Surely, he was done screwing up for the night.

"How about the taco special?" Ash suggested.

"Sounds good," he managed.

The server walked away.

Silence.

He stared at Ash, feeling like he was meeting her for the first time all over again. She was beautiful—even more so as a woman than she'd been as a teen, and she'd stolen his breath and ability to think then. But it was more than that. It was the way she loved him. Her sweetness and her fire. She was smart and kind and fun to be with. And her soul was generous. She never failed to jump into any project to help.

And she'd supported him always.

Time to man up and be the man she wanted and needed.

"Beck, you're staring."

"I love looking at you."

She seemed irritated by the compliment.

"You're making this harder than it has to be," she said.

"I don't want to," he said seriously. "Well, I do because I don't want to break up," he admitted. "But I do want to support your new goals. I just feel blindsided."

She opened her mouth, no doubt to object. But then she closed it again. He waited. Nothing, only Ashni fidgeting in her seat.

"You never talked to me about your feelings," he began, cautiously tempering the spark of hope. "You didn't tell me you weren't enjoying your job or that you were tired of traveling and wanting to put down roots."

She looked stricken.

"How was I supposed to know?" He inherently pressed his new advantage.

"Beck, it's too late to go into this now."

Too late? This was just the beginning. Ben Ballantyne hadn't raised quitters, and Beck wasn't ceding the most important fight of his life.

"I'm not absolving myself of anything. It takes two to make a relationship work and I've not been supporting you like you needed."

Ash pressed her lips together. Half stood. Then sat down.

"Don't do this," she whispered. "It's too late. I broke up with you." Her voice shook. "I have to make a life for myself."

His heart ached for her. For him.

"Ashni, I want you to have the life you want. I do. I just want us to build and live that life together. If you feel that I haven't been taking care of your needs, let me support you now. Tell me what you want. Tell me what you need. I want to be your support and cheerleader as you've been mine for so many years. It's your turn." He could just imagine if Bodhi could see him now. He'd be full of unsolicited advice and caustic reviews.

She shook her head. "That doesn't make any sense. That's not fair to you. We want vastly different things in life."

He wanted her. His family. The ranch. None of it would work without her.

"Tell me what you want. Tell me what you need," he repeated. He could make it work. Anything for her.

She bit down so hard on her lip that he was afraid she'd draw blood.

"It may take two to make a relationship work," Ashni said, drawing strength from somewhere, because her eyes seemed to spark as she stood and tossed one vibrant end of her scarf over her shoulder. "But it only takes one to make it fail. I want out. You need to accept that. Don't try to trick me into seeing you again. You didn't want closure. You're not worried about your granddad."

Ashni walked out the door just as the server arrived with the two plates. His instinct was to chase after her, but he kept his butt planted in his chair and picked up a taco. "I'll need a box and the check please," he said firmly, watching

Ash cross the street.

Marietta was safe, but he wanted to make sure she made it home. She was still his to love and protect.

"Son, you gonna chase her?" an old-timer who'd been sitting two booths away and had gotten up after leaving money on his table during Ash's slap down now asked looking pointedly at Beck.

"I'm going to catch her," he vowed as her hair flared out behind her like a banner.

ASHNI HURRIED BACK to the apartment that already felt more like home than the way too many standard-issue hotel rooms she'd stayed in with Beck. And it was a palace compared to his rig.

She'd loved the adventure until it seemed to have no end date, and she had seemed to be just one more accessory he packed away.

At least Beck hadn't chased after her. She'd jogged home expecting to hear him running or his truck the entire way. Weird that he'd let her go like that.

You're supposed to be happy he stayed put.

But she didn't feel happy. Her emotions were all over the place lately. She shouldn't have met him. That had been weak. She justified it because she was worried about Ben, but Ashni was more worried that she'd wanted to meet Beck because she missed him and was curious about what he might try.

Not something she was proud of.

Or that she could allow herself to repeat.

Her phone buzzed.

Beck.

She wasn't even going to look. Except she did. A local number.

"Hello, this is Ashni Singh."

"Hi, Ashni. I hope I am not calling too late. My name is Dr. Saria Conte. I'm the director of Crawford County's public health department. I have your résumé, and you answered my email earlier this afternoon."

"Oh. Wow. That was fast." She slowly lowered herself onto the small sofa and kicked off her sandals.

"That probably gives away how eager I am to fill the position." Saria laughed but sounded a bit wry. "Since one important piece of the job position is as a liaison with the public schools, which started up a few weeks ago."

"Yes, the public-school aspect of the job really appealed to me. I have done a lot of outreach with the pro rodeo tour with children's organizations and the children's hospitals in the tour's cities for the past five years." Ash suddenly felt breathless.

Was she really doing this?

"I wanted to set up an interview time with you."

"Great. What time works for you?" She shrugged out of her jacket, suddenly feeling a bit warm and constrained. She unwrapped her scarf and draped it over the back of the couch.

She had a job interview. An interview in the field where she'd received her master's. It was a job that didn't require travel outside the county except perhaps an occasional meeting in the state capital in Helena.

She was teaching an art class.

She was moving on with her life.

She was newly single.

That last thought didn't spark the joy of the first two on the list. *Dumb heart.* Loving Beck was habit. She could break it.

"Do you have any time available tomorrow or Wednesday?"

"Yes." Ash jumped up and danced around the studio. "Morning would be best if possible," she said. "I'm volunteering at Harry's House this week and teaching an after-school art class."

"I am not surprised," Dr. Conte said. "All the volunteer hours with children on your résumé as well as your master's focus on community health outreach with families jumped out at me. Are you okay with meeting me fairly early?"

"Of course."

"Good. I'll bring the coffee. Is eight thirty at the public health department tomorrow okay? Our offices are near the hospital."

Definitely walkable. "Yes, that's perfect."

That didn't seem early at all. Probably because she and Beck were always up with or before the sun—ranch hours, he called them.

Stop thinking of Beck.

She ended the call and swallowed hard, pretending that she didn't feel the lump in her throat, the pressure on her chest or tears burning her eyes.

"I'm happy," she told the empty room defiantly.

She was reinventing herself and her life. And Beck needed to stay in her rearview mirror until she learned how to deal with him without wanting him.

Anticlimatically, her stomach rumbled. She'd been so wound up about seeing Beck she hadn't even eaten a chip. And she'd walked away just as dinner had arrived. She glared at the kitchen cupboards where she'd stored the few staples she'd bought with Sky yesterday as if it was the cupboards' fault she was too tired to cook.

The tap on her door was light.

Of course. Beck. She should have known he'd never let her walk home alone or have the last word.

She swung open her front door, ready to verbally spar. This had to stop.

Beck leaned against her doorjamb, looking deliciously casual.

"Dinner." He handed her a Rosita's bag plus an extra bag of their chips and a container of their house-made salsa and another of guac.

"Oh." She felt petty. "Thank you."

She nearly backed up to let him in but managed to quell the urge.

"Do you want the food?" he asked looking at her death grip on the doorjamb.

"Um. Yeah. Thanks." She peeled her fingers off the wood and took the bags and stacked containers.

"You have a good night now." He leaned forward and his lips brushed her cheek, and before she could even process his familiar scent and the warmth of his lips, he was gone, hurrying down the steps and back out into the night.

Chapter Eight

"You going to chase her?"

The question from last night still rang in his memory and mocked him.

Heck yeah, he was going to chase her. But all he seemed to be doing lately was standing still, even as he kept himself busier than usual at the ranch. He'd spent all of Tuesday checking and repairing fencing with Cade Osterfeld, a ranch hand who'd worked and lived on the ranch for more than a decade. Cade was quiet, and Beck had appreciated the quiet to think and plan.

He'd also—for the first time he could remember—wanted to be away from his cousins.

If he had to listen to Bodhi's offers of seduction tips or Ashni sightings like the one where Bodhi had seen her sitting in the sun, face tilted to the sky, sipping a hot chocolate from Sage's Copper Mountain Chocolate Shop, Bodhi was going to end up with a black eye or a hole in his beautiful, lady-killer smile.

"You're ceding the field," Bodhi had said. "Giving Ash too much lead."

Meanwhile, Bodhi and Bowen seemed to be neck and

neck in their Rodeo Bride Game. Bodhi had brought Nico to the ranch for a picnic lunch and horse ride, and Bowen had done the same with Langston. Beck had worked until long after sundown with the moms' list of directions that he had carried out without complaint.

Bowen, his mom, and Langston had started decorating the barn now that it had been emptied, repaired and repainted. Bodhi and Nico had concentrated on cleaning and fixing up the log cabin on Plum Hill. Beck felt more like a landscaper than a cowboy this week as he worked with the hired crew landscaping around the main house and helping with some upgrades inside including refinishing the floors. The house, the yard and Plum Hill and North Vista barn had never looked more beautiful, but it just made him feel more and more like he was standing on quicksand. Usually it would have been he and Ash working side by side preparing for the Bash. His mom had shrugged off Ash's absence, hands on her skinny hips.

"Good for her," his mom had said when her sister Genevieve had finally asked about Ashni. "Girl finally found some sense. She's been following you around like a puppy since you were both kids. She always was far too talented and smart to live her life through you, staring at the ribbons of road like the brokenhearted star of a mournful country song." Beck's mom had always spoken her mind in great detail. "Ashni was intending to go to medical school. Instead she became your professional girlfriend."

Beck had been appalled. Ash was so much more than a

girlfriend. She'd decided against medical school years ago.

Because you'd be separated too much.

But she'd accomplished so much for the tour's marketing department. She'd created many community outreach programs and had built up the social media presence exponentially. She'd been full of ideas and had loved it.

Until she hadn't.

It had been like this for three days. Him feeling like he had a hole in his chest the size of his boot. Giving Ash the space she wanted and hating every minute of it. Working from dawn past sundown but finding no peace in the exhaustion. And searching for and finding answers he didn't like. His mom was right. Ashni had followed him. Lived his dream.

And now she wanted to follow her own.

So today, Wednesday, as he'd been loading hay bales and arranging them up in the loft of Vista Barn after doing a deep clean of the entire barn since he'd helped repair the roof, he'd sat down on a hay bale and stared out of the upper door toward Copper Mountain. It was his favorite place in the world. It was where he and Ash had first made love many years ago. And where he'd first told her that he wanted to build a home for them on Plum Hill and raise their family alongside his granddad, and his cousins and their families. All of them would continue to build the ranch for the next generation.

"I'll be happy anywhere as long as we're together," she'd told him, skin gleaming in the light slanting through the barn.

She'd lost that belief in them. Or he'd killed it through inattention.

And all the turmoil that had been churning inside him settled. He knew what he had to do.

She was done following him, and so it was his turn to follow her. Let her chase her dream. And he'd build his own with her. Only the thought of perhaps not having the ranch as his home base made him feel utterly lost. He still couldn't believe his granddad was contemplating selling. It wasn't yet a done deal, at least it wouldn't feel done until Beck saw a sale sign, but so far his granddad had refused to talk about the ranch or the future with him or with either of his cousins, and they'd all tried. Beck didn't know what the future held, but he knew what he had to do.

Beck pulled out his phone and composed a short email telling the tour that after the finals, he would be retiring. He could have saved it to drafts. Discussed the momentous decisions with his granddad or his cousins. Shared it with Ash and have her look over the wording to see if there was a way to make it better, but in the end, he just wanted to be his own man and keep his own counsel.

He'd pushed send.

That night, just as the sun was setting, Beck stood on the back porch and grilled the steaks and veggies. The night was so mild, they were going to sit outside on the large outdoor patio for dinner. Everyone but Ash would be together for dinner. He still felt pulled apart. But his decision felt right.

He wanted to tell Ash the news, but what if it weren't enough of a declaration for her? What if he didn't have the ranch to work and on which to craft a future with her?

One worry at a time.

His granddad always said that, only Beck had more than one worry.

Ben Ballantyne came out on the back porch to check the fire he'd built in the outdoor fireplace. They'd rebuilt and expanded the outdoor patio five years ago and had added the stone chimney, which Ash had had the idea to make into a double fireplace so people could be around the patio under cover or under the stars and still have a fire. Everything came back to Ash for him. She was bone-deep. He didn't know how he'd make a life without her. So many memories. Part of his DNA.

But did she still feel the same? Did she miss him?

"Those steaks about done?" Granddad asked, still poking a little at the roaring fire.

"Getting there." Beck's voice creaked like he was fifteen again.

God, everything was just so off. The Montana Rodeo Bride Game had gone too far, pitting him and his cousins against each other in a way they never had. He couldn't be honest about his feelings and concerns about Ash because it was a competition, and if Ash was done with him, there was one less player on the field. They wouldn't care that Beck felt destroyed—his future whisked away by his own hesitation that he'd be a screwup at love like his mom. And then there was his greedy desire to best his cousins' points. He'd always been chasing them, chasing his own glory. And he'd dragged Ash along on his endless quest.

The truth about his part in the breakup sledgehammered him.

Even the family dinner, which should have sparked joy, had become part of the game, with Bodhi and Bowen inviting the women they were "seeing."

And no one was grieving Ash not being with them. No one but him.

"Looks good." Granddad joined him at the grill.

"Granddad." He took the plunge again. "What made you start thinking about selling the ranch? You've lived here all your life."

"Just because I've done one thing doesn't mean I can't do another."

"But..." Beck stared at his granddad's angular profile, and then his gaze dropped down to his hands, still strong, rough, spotted with age. "The ranch is you. It's your life." He struggled to put all of his feelings in a coherent sentence.

"My family is my life," his granddad said kindly. "I'd like to be closer to y'all."

"But—" He broke off. How would they be close with everyone scattered and no home to gather in?

"Keep your eyes on the steaks," his granddad said. "Plenty of time for gazing into the future after the Bash. Even polished my crystal ball for the occasion. Chin up, Beck. You'll find your path."

His granddad didn't need a crystal ball to read his mind. Beck only hoped he was right.

⭐

ASHNI HAD DECIDED to rent a car to give herself more freedom and flexibility, and as she drove out to the Wilder ranch Wednesday night, her mind reeled. She was thrilled that Sky had texted her and asked her to dinner, because she didn't want to be alone with her thoughts.

How was it possible to be excited and terrified at the same time?

On Tuesday morning, she'd interviewed for the job at the public health department. This morning, she'd been offered the job and had accepted it. She'd talked to Walker Wilder about renting the studio apartment for a little longer to give herself time to find a new place and settle into her new life.

New life. Something she'd wanted. Only it felt like she was moving crazy fast. Ashni looked at the speedometer as she drove down Highway 89. Yup. Fast. She eased off the gas a little. She was going to need to buy a car. Rent an apartment. No. A small home. She'd make a garden next spring.

What was she doing? She was changing her entire life in a couple of days, and it felt illicit. She'd told no one. Not Beck. Not her parents. Not Reeva. It felt like she'd been in a bubble since Sunday, isolated from everyone and floating up, up, and away. When would it pop?

At least she had Sky to run things by. Once on Wilder land, Ashni drove past the cluster of houses and a large barn and on to a smaller pole barn that served as Sky's main studio and forge. Sky stood outside the studio. Ashni had toured the studio yesterday, in awe and already she was thinking about how she would have more space now, and she could incorporate art back into her life.

"Hey." Sky hugged her. "You look wind-blown and radiant. You must have good news."

"I got it."

Sky whooped. Danced in a circle and hugged her again. "You're staying! Fantastic. Is Beck freaking out?"

And Ashni plunged back to earth. "I…ahhh—" she played with a button on her denim jacket "—haven't told him yet."

Sky didn't immediately respond. Ashni liked that about her. She was thoughtful. She gave Ashni time to think things through whereas Beck always jumped into problem solving mode, and her mom looked to cast the blame.

"Well, I'm excited. And definitely not surprised you got it. You'll be great as a community and school health department liaison. I bet you already are getting ideas for how to change things up."

Ashni nodded. Not that she knew too much yet about the job, but she had researched what the position entailed and what other counties in Montana were doing before she'd gone for the interview.

"Let's go to the house and get some iced tea or something a bit stronger if you want before dinner," Sky said, linking arms with her.

Ashni liked that too. Sky reminded her of Reeva—she was wide open and physically affectionate.

They walked along the birch-tree-lined gravel road back toward the house. Sky looked thoughtful but also pale—more pale than usual.

"You okay?"

"Yes." Sky flashed a smile that looked a bit rueful. She sighed. "I've had some news myself. Good news, but I wouldn't have minded not having it for another year or so."

Sky laughed—probably at Ashni's bewilderment. They arrived at the outdoor living space that the four homes on the ranch shared when they all got together. It was a large patio with a sitting area and a fire pit and then another covered area that had an outdoor kitchen and fridge and several picnic tables. Outdoor lights swooped in several rows along the beams of the covered area and stretched out to connect to large beams of what looked like reclaimed lumber on the opposite of the patio.

The massive grill was heating up, but nothing was on it yet.

"We're having fish tonight," Sky said. "A couple of the boys went fishing this morning and were as usual hyper successful. That's how I knew for certain."

Ashni's nose wrinkled in confusion.

Sky laughed again and then she went to the fridge. "Someone went on a beer run." She pulled out a large container of sun tea. "I made this, this morning. Would you like some tea, or there's pretty much a convenience store full of other things." Sky swung the door wide so that Ashni could see the collection of flavored sparkling waters, soda, beer, and several white wines.

"The tea sounds great."

Everything else sounded awful.

Sky poured two glasses of the tea and sliced a lemon.

"Your class is half done," Sky commented as she sat down on the opposite side of one of the picnic tables. "Are you still enjoying it?"

"Loving it," Ashni admitted. "It's going really smoothly. The kids are really sparking with ideas and collaborating—even helping each other when they run into a problem. And we'll hit our timeline, which was an initial concern."

"Fantastic, cheers." Sky clinked glasses with hers. "Now that you're going to stay, you can teach another class if you want, either a once-a-week club class or another workshop on one of the breaks."

"Staying," Ashni mused. "That sounds so good."

"Montana and I traveled with Kane off and on for a year when he was doing the American Extreme Bull Riding Tour. I loved exploring the new cities, getting to know the other riders and their families and the tour staff."

"I loved it too the first couple of years." Ashni sipped at her tea. "But it just got old and this year I just felt done and worried Beck wouldn't ever want to quit touring and competing. That was never our plan. He said one year, two tops if he was winning. But it just kept going, and he kept winning. This past year he didn't even consult me about re-upping. I don't know what would get him to quit except if his cousins did…or a real bad injury," she whispered, scared to utter the word.

"Rodeo is not for the faint of heart—not for cowboys or those who love them."

"I'm trying not to love him."

"It's not that easy," Sky said. "And why would you let go so easily? Give yourself this time to start to build a life and let him realize how much you are a part of his. He can head out without you and get a feel for the road alone."

That's what Ashni hoped even though she didn't want to.

Sky's voice was warm and soothing, but Ashni wanted to change the subject. She ran her tongue along her upper lip. "Pomegranate tea? Hibiscus?"

"You have an excellent palate."

"I didn't used to," Ashni said. "Lately, it's like I'm a giant nose."

Sky, who'd stood up to grab one of the baguettes that was upright with a few other loaves of bread paused, gave her a funny look and then wielded a bread knife and began slicing.

"You never told me your news," Ashni prompted.

Sky brought over a bowl with sliced baguette and then some butter, knives and a small bowl of olive oil and fig vinegar. She sat down.

"Dinner won't be for another hour, and I want a snack." Sky buttered her round of baguette, popped the whole thing in her mouth, and closed her eyes.

"This is about all I'm going to be able to eat soon," she said eyes still closed as she chewed. "I'm pregnant."

Ashni blinked. "Congratulations. Right?" she asked after Sky didn't answer.

"Yes. Definitely. Kane and I want a big family, but I have a couple of big commissions coming up, so we were going to wait a year. I'd actually had an appointment with my ob-gyn to discuss different birth control options and then Monday I had a crazy vivid dream and…"

"Vivid dream?" Ashni parroted, eyes wide as she thought about her Beck dreams over the past couple of restless weeks. Beck. Bright. Loud. Laughing. And out of reach. She'd barely been able to sleep during the two weeks at Reeva's wedding preparation. Her dreams had been disturbingly loud, weird and colorful and had woken her up repeatedly.

Ashni nibbled on her thumbnail.

"And then there's my enhanced sense of smell. I love coffee, but now it smells awful. And when the boys brought the fish home to clean it, I nearly lost it. That sealed the deal."

Ashni stood up. No. Not happening. She'd always been imaginative. But this was over the top even for her.

"Maybe you aren't."

"After three, I know. I took a test this afternoon. Kane's over the moon thinking he's all that. I swear that man is so potent he can knock me up from across a room."

But Ashni didn't laugh.

I can't be.

I'm not.

She pushed the suspicion away.

This would be epically poor timing.

She wasn't pregnant. Nope. No way. She couldn't be. She wouldn't be. But even as she rejected the possibility, she remembered how off she'd felt the entire time of Reeva's wedding. She hadn't felt hungry because her stomach had felt uneasy. And most things had smelled or tasted unappealing.

"I can't be," she whispered to Sky. "Not now."

She'd wanted to start a family with Beck for a couple of years.

"We're broken up."

She was rebuilding her life. She'd just accepted a new job today.

"When was your last period?"

Yes. Her period. A rush of relief surged through her, which immediately turned to doom.

"Ahhh, it was really light," she said. "Not much. But I was stressed. Working extra so I could take off time for my cousin's wedding and then the week in Marietta. And…the Beck issue." She'd been struggling, wanting something Beck wasn't ready to give.

Maybe he never would be.

But if she were pregnant…

Ashni crossed her arms tightly over her chest. "This is

bad."

Sky got up and came around the table, sitting beside her. She hugged her and Ashni, who'd been trying so hard to hold herself together this week, hugged her back, tears flowing.

"Is it bad? Didn't you and Beck ever talk about starting a family?"

"I did. He brushed it off. I think his mom did a number on him. He doesn't talk about it much, but she married and divorced four times before he left for college."

"Four?" Sky's mouth dropped comically.

"I know."

"But you and Beck have been together since high school, so maybe it's just the rodeo. He wants to focus on his career because it's such a short one."

The rodeo.

Ashni wiped at her tears, embarrassed. She didn't know Sky all that well, but she really liked her and felt they could become close friends.

What was she going to do? She was just finding her feet, taking baby steps and now this: a baby. But Sky balanced motherhood with her career.

I will too.

She bit down on her lip. Sky had Kane. And a large family. She'd be alone.

Ashni tried to corral her panic. She was making a huge leap. Maybe she wasn't even pregnant. The pinprick of disappointment following that thought was dismaying. She and Beck were broken up. She shouldn't want to be pregnant. She'd just cut Beck loose to live his life while she lived hers. No way did she want to spring this surprise on him. The visual of his discomfort as Jerry pressed him about his plans swam into view.

Her impulse was to head to the store, buy a test and take it. Instead she dragged in a deep breath in an attempt to calm down. She'd been invited to dinner with all of Sky's extended family in Marietta, and she was going to stay and enjoy herself. She wanted a life rich with friends, and this week was her start.

"Ashni, are you freaking out?"

"I should be." She picked up her iced tea and pressed the cold glass against her forehead. "But I'm not going to. I might not be pregnant." Wow, that word sounded alien coming out of her mouth. She'd spent the last decade determined to not get pregnant. "Beck and I are always very careful."

"Yeah. So were Kane and I," Sky said ruefully, looking down at her still-flat stomach. "But some cowboys just got good game, and science cannot win against that."

"Beck better not be one of them."

Chapter Nine

Beck was.

The next morning Ashni stared at the blue "pregnant" line for who knows how long. Then she put the test down and made herself a chai. She sat down on the top step of the studio apartment and stared at the large oak tree in the yard that shaded an outdoor patio space and then lifted her gaze farther to stare down Bramble Lane.

She felt eerily calm. Usually, her mind raced with plans, ideas, things to do. This morning, as dawn crept over the black, star-studded sky and turned it a pinky gray her mind was blissfully silent.

She finished her chai, her hands cupping the mug for warmth, and waited for it to get light enough so that she could go for her morning run. How long would she be able to run? She'd need to buy a jogger.

"So much for a quiet mind." She laughed at herself.

She got back up and went inside. She looked at the test again. Still pregnant. She stripped off her clothes and looked at herself in the full-length mirror. She looked the same. She touched her breasts. They were tender, aching a little. Her stomach was still taut—a little ripped as she liked to work out. That wouldn't last long. She touched her muscle definition.

What was she going to do?

The pregnancy wouldn't change her plans. She would still stay in Marietta and take the job. She'd have to tell her new boss. That was only fair. And her parents. Her eyes widened in panic. And Beck. She'd have to tell him. Oh. God. This was a disaster.

"You're changing everything," she accused, but her palm, which had flattened over her abdomen spread out, and wonder seeped through her panic.

She was going to be a mother.

A single mother. Not a concept she'd ever thought would ever relate to her because she'd always had Beck. Beck who hadn't contacted her since Monday night. He'd left her alone as she'd asked except to send tacos and chips and salsa for her class on Tuesday. And cookies from the Copper Mountain Gingerbread and Dessert Company on Wednesday. What would he send today, pacifiers? Sippy cups?

She'd tell him after the rodeo. He didn't need the distraction, and she had to come to terms with it so she didn't panic and cling to him, launching herself back into his life.

Unnerved by her thoughts, Ash dressed in her leggings, a sports bra, long-sleeve Nike zip-up tee, and running shoes. A hard run would settle her. She'd figure out how to tell Beck—after the rodeo.

She left the apartment. The spit dried in her mouth.

Beck stood at the bottom of the stairs, dressed in running

shorts and a wicking tee that hugged his shoulders and pecs. Her mouth opened. He stretched as if nothing in the world had changed between them.

"Thought I'd join you."

He looked so beautiful—his face a little leaner, his gaze more somber than she'd ever seen it except when a cowboy on the tour had been seriously and permanently injured, and they'd visited him in the hospital and his pregnant wife had been there openly weeping while he'd been sleeping off the anesthetic from the surgery that hadn't been guaranteed to ensure he'd ever walk again.

That could be Beck someday.

"Ash?"

Even his voice sounded deeper, darker, and whispered through her heating her blood in a way that was all too familiar.

In answer, she took off at a dead run.

THIS HAD BEEN an interesting morning, Beck thought after a five-mile run that had seemed more like a race.

"I have an outdoor shower." Walker Wilder poked her head out of one of her French doors. "It's more for dogs, but I make Calum clean up out there sometimes when he puts in a messy shift at the raptor rescue center out near Bozeman. Water's heated."

"Thanks." He waved at her, a bit embarrassed that he'd

been caught shirtless after the run and hosing off in her driveway probably before she'd knocked back her first coffee.

"It's more private." Walker smirked. "Not that I minded the show, but Calum's getting ticked that I'm googly eying you."

"No, I'm not." Calum joined his wife at the door and wrapped his arms around her and his hands cupped her very large, very low baby bump. Women were amazing, nurturing life inside of them. And how the heck did their skin and muscles stretch out that much?

If Ash ever got pregnant, he'd be a nervous wreck.

"I took a few pictures and posted them on the Copper Mountain Rodeo site."

Beck turned off the hose and dried off with his T-shirt.

"And then I posted to my Ghost Quest site that I spotted an exhibitionist spirit in my yard. Pretty pale there, cowboy. Find some sun."

They closed the door, still laughing at him. Yeah, that's what he had time to do with Ashni kicking his backside to the curb, the moms descending and riding his ass with a million chores to prepare the ranch and house for a party and imminent sale, and his granddad acting out of sorts and contemplating selling his ranch and leaving Marietta forever—relax for a few days on a beach.

He grabbed his jeans and shirt from his truck, found the shower, and washed off quick. Ash had improbably agreed to have breakfast with him at Main Street Diner, and he didn't want to give her a reason to change her mind.

He'd showed restraint worthy of a UN diplomat for not contacting her for several days. He'd wanted to. A million texts had run through his mind. Pictures he could have taken with funny captions that would have made her laugh or remind her of special moments. The whole ranch was one giant memory—more with her than growing up with his cousins. She couldn't be out of his life. It would be like cutting off his arm.

He'd sent food to the kids and only one picture—no caption. A hale bale in the loft of the barn that he'd covered with a red and white eyelet plaid slipcover, that he'd positioned to look out of the barn's loft window.

It was their spot. They'd made love there. Sure. But so much more. Some evenings they'd just sit, watch the sun go down, hold each other, talk about nothing and everything, and sometimes she'd play her guitar and sing.

He had to win her back. Had to. And it had nothing to do with Bodhi's damn game and everything to do with Ash. The tour had emailed him back asking him if he was sure he didn't want to re-up for next year. He was. They said he could change his mind until after the Christmas holidays. His agent had emailed back to say he was crazy. His endorsements would dry up. Beck didn't care.

He'd win his girl back and rebuild his life starting with her, with or without the ranch.

He dressed quickly and sat on top of a picnic table to wait. Arguments and words bombarded his mind. He just needed the right combo to persuade her, but even as she opened the door—stealing his breath in her dark skinny jeans, paisley-printed tunic top with embroidered flowers on it, and her hair tumbling freely down to the small of her back—he hadn't settled on what to say.

He just wanted to kiss her.

She flicked one end of her long, silky scarf nervously over her shoulder.

"I'm ready," she said softly looking anything but.

They walked to the Main Street Diner. He'd hoped to drive her and convince her to come out to the ranch to see all the work he'd been doing, but Ashni said she had some things to do at Harry's House, and his spirits—soaring because she'd gone on a run with him, dipped. Would she even come to the party?

Flo greeted them. Took their breakfast order. Ashni ordered yogurt and fruit and toast. Beck loaded up on the protein. He had a busy morning ahead and was moving Raider to the rodeo grounds later in the afternoon.

Flo brought the coffee and tea, but Ashni still hadn't said anything. Her gaze pinged around the room, but she was all that held his attention.

"Ashni, whatever it is, we can make it right. Together," he said, his hands capturing hers as she fiddled with her cutlery.

She finally looked at him.

"I promise. I'll do whatever it takes." He meant it. Wanted her to see that he meant it.

"I'm pregnant."

Millions of men had been slapped upside the head with that word. He was only one more. There was probably an appropriate response. A safe one. A twenty-first-century self-actualized male response, but Beck had no idea what it was.

What? How? When?

Stupid questions. Irrelevant questions so he clamped his mouth shut. Was this why she'd been acting so weird? Relief coursed through him, warring with shock.

She kept watching him, wary and defiant.

The defiance threw him. Had she gone off birth control on purpose? That was so un-Ash-like that he dismissed the suspicion immediately. Besides, it was irrelevant. The baby was his. Ash was his.

A response was required. "How are you feeling?" he asked carefully. It seemed the safest option of everything screaming in his brain.

Damn, but he couldn't breathe. And he felt sweaty and prickingly hot. He should have stuck with the hose. That icy glacier-fed water had damn near frozen his balls off—probably something Ash would appreciate right about now.

"Weird. Crappy." She stirred honey in her tea, seemingly calmer just as his freak-out was ramping up.

"How…how long?" He winced. Totally stupid question. Pregnant was all or nothing. A week or a month didn't make a woman any more pregnant.

"I don't know. Maybe a few weeks. Or more."

"Or more?" he echoed. "How can you not know? Why are you just telling me now?"

"Keep your voice down." She scanned the busy restaurant. "I'd prefer to announce the news with an ad in the *Courier*," she said sarcastically.

"We never should have gone for that run," he burst out. He hadn't been protecting her. He hadn't been protecting their child because he hadn't known! "Why are you just telling me now?" he demanded.

"I was going to wait until after the rodeo. I didn't want you distracted, but it's all I could think of this morning. Even the run didn't clear my mind."

"Why the hell would you sit on news like this?"

"Calm down," she urged. "It's not like me being pregnant changes anything."

"Like hell it doesn't. It changes everything."

Ash shook her head, quick, hard. Beck dropped her hands like they were stove-hot.

"We're still broken up," she said calmly as if she weren't aiming a Marlin Model 336 rifle at his chest. "In fact—"

"We are not broken up. You're pregnant."

By now a few people were looking. Beck didn't care.

"I am not marrying you because of a baby," she hissed.

"Too bad. I am not *not* marrying the mother of my child. You're being ridiculous." He busted his leash on calm twenty-first-century male. "Stop playing games. First, you're pissed that I don't ask you to marry me, and now you say you won't marry me when you're pregnant. We are going to be parents, and I take that seriously. I am not walking away from my responsibility."

Ash launched up, eyes spitting fire. "I am not marrying a jackass cowboy who thinks of me as a responsibility. I can take care of myself and my baby."

She shrugged back into her cropped denim jacket and fluffed her hair so that it swung around her angry face like a dark cloud of doom. She kept her voice low, but each word was a precisely articulated bullet.

"For your information, Beck Ballantyne, you're the last man I'd marry. When I do marry, *if* I marry—" she stressed the *if* like that was going to impress him "—I'm going to marry a man who adores me. A man who can't wait to share his life with me. A man who doesn't want to go one more day without me as his wife. And I definitely am not going to marry a man in a quickie courthouse ceremony. When I marry, my family will be there. I will have a red sari and a white dress. I will celebrate *jaimala* in front of my family and friends. I will have a *sangeet* party with mehndi and singing and dancing and food. I will have a ceremony with vows that my future husband and I write to each other, and we will make promises to each other in front of God and everyone. And I will be loved and happy and build a home and a life with the man of my dreams, who doesn't see me as one more chore he's got to take care of. And my baby will know it's loved, not one more thing grudgingly scrawled on a to-do list."

Ash grabbed her purse, tossed her scarf gracefully over her shoulder, and swept out of the restaurant.

And for the second time in one week—that had to be

some sort of a record, didn't it?—Beck watched Ashni walk away from another meal and him while a man he didn't know in the booth behind him asked, "Son, you gonna go chase after your baby mama?"

"Nope," Beck said feeling strangely sanguine and pissed at the same time. He picked up his coffee and watched Flo approach with two breakfasts. Good. He was hungry. "I already caught her. Just thinking of the best way to reel her back in."

"It's Friday night," Bodhi sang out and executed a dance move that kicked up fresh sawdust.

Christ, after another day of hard labor that lasted late into the night, and finally receiving a terse 'we both need time to process' text from Ashni after he'd called and texted several times throughout the day, he'd again been unable to sleep. He'd spent the time researching Montana's marriage license requirements and diamonds online. Beck was not in the mood for Bodhi's playfulness.

He and his cousins were about to load up their horses and head to the fairgrounds.

"Look at you, all grumpy because you've been getting none." Bodhi laughed.

"Bodhi." Bowen's voice was low. But it had that tone. The tone that usually stopped everything and everyone dead in its tracks.

But not this time.

"Maybe it's time to switch horses mid-ride, Mr. All Flapping Jaw But No Action," Bodhi taunted.

Beck didn't even remember moving. Next thing he knew he was breathing hard, Bowen had flipped him over his shoulder and had him in a headlock, and Bodhi was getting up off the ground, his mouth bleeding and a bruise already coming up high on his cheek.

"Damn. That was fast." Bodhi, as usual, seemed wryly amused. "Haven't seen you move like that since you were fourteen and I asked—"

"What the fuck is wrong with you?" Bowen strong-armed Bodhi across the barn. "For once, zip it."

Bodhi picked up his hat and slapped off the dust. "Zipped." He smirked.

"We good?" Bowen asked.

No. Beck was anything but good.

He was going to be a father.

And the mother of his baby didn't want anything to do with him.

And he couldn't even share his good news because it wasn't good yet since Ash said he was the last man she'd marry. And his family seemed intent on beautifying the ranch to offload it on a celebrity or multi-millionaire who wouldn't appreciate the heritage. Beck's child might never sit atop Plum Hill or swim in the creek or learn to ride over the endless fields of Three Tree Ranch.

Bodhi had another bruise coming up along his jaw.

"Sorry," Beck muttered. He hadn't realized he'd hit that hard. He just remembered seeing white as everything buzzed out. He had to pull himself together.

"Is that a sorry, not sorry?" Bodhi grinned and held out his hand to be slapped. Hard. It had been that way since they were kids. Bodhi's idea, of course. He could never do anything the normal way, not even a handshake.

"Mid-way to a real sorry. I was hoping a true love relationship, even a fake one, would improve you, but no such luck."

Bodhi's cocky grin faded. Steel entered his gaze.

Interesting.

"No such luck." Bodhi repeated and eloquently shrugged his shoulders. "Damn, I think you got in five or six punches before Bowen put your ass down." Bodhi adjusted his body as if to see if it still worked. "Getting slow in your old age," he said to Bowen. "You used to pull him off before he got in two."

"Why's that my job?" Bowen was his usual laconic self. "You just stood there, mouth hanging open like the target everyone wants to take a swing at."

"Everyone's got a talent. Pissing off friends and family is mine," Bodhi said. "But hey, if this rodeo thing doesn't work out, consider cage fighting, Beck." He sauntered toward the barn door, a hitch in his normally fluid stride, and guilt flooded Beck.

"You good?" Bowen called after him.

Bodhi whistled a Rascal Flatts tune and pushed the barn

doors wide open to make it easier to load their horses.

"How 'bout you?" Bowen demanded.

No.

But determination flooded him. Ash was his world. They were having a baby. He was a Marietta ranch cowboy to his bones no matter what his birth certificate said.

"I'll get there." He stomped down the urge to share the news about the baby. It was something they should share with their families together, and he had no inclination to let his unborn child become part of Bodhi and Bowen's dumb Rodeo Bride Game. He wasn't playing. His proposal to Ash would be private. His commitment would have no strings. Nothing on the line but his love for her and their life together.

The ranch might be gone forever for him, but he'd have his wife and child and that was everything. Ash and their baby were his future.

ASHNI SAT CROSS-LEGGED on one of the desks and stared at her phone. Reeva had texted to ask how she was. She'd been posting pictures of her honeymoon regularly on her Instagram account, and Ashni had dutifully thumbs-upped and commented, but what to do with this latest text. She'd told Reeva everything. All her secrets. All her feelings about Beck. All her hopes and dreams.

But not that she'd been unhappy this year.

Even as Reeva had found John, Ashni had been losing herself and Beck.

But she couldn't not respond so she thumbed through her photos and shared a few of the mural and the kids, whose parents had signed photo releases so she could post on Harry's House's website.

But she didn't tell her about the baby.

Or that she and Beck had broken up.

She felt so alone and isolated. And she still had a few hours until class started.

"Hey, girl." Sky breezed in. "I'm on my way to teach at the college, but I wanted to check in and see how you're feeling. And I brought the elixir of the gods."

"Wine?" She wouldn't be having a late harvest Riesling or a Pinot Blanc for a really long time now. She remembered the whiskey shot Sunday night guiltily.

"We're both cut off," Sky said cheerfully. She held up two to-go cups from Copper Mountain Chocolate. "This is even better."

It was. Usually. Ashni had needed to be really careful about what she ate lately because so many things disagreed with her, which should have been a clue, but no. Some public health expert she was. She didn't know jack about her own body.

"Thank you." She sniffed at the rich chocolate scent, and her mouth watered. She lifted the lid and scooped out some whipped cream with her finger and licked it off.

She sighed. Delicious. She could survive on Sage's hot

chocolate for the next however many months.

"So when are you going to tell Beck?" Sky asked.

"I was going to wait until after the rodeo. I just wanted to have some time to think and process and come to terms with the news."

Sky nodded.

"But then I blurted it out at the Main Street Diner. Really, I'm surprised the entire town doesn't know by now. I was not subtle, and I swanned out like a pop star noticing there hadn't been a sound check and ever worse lighting." She rolled her eyes.

Sky's eyes were huge. "How did Beck take the news?"

"Awful. He thinks we should get married at the courthouse immediately."

"Yup." Sky grinned. "I had that pegged right. I know my cowboys. Players and all about fun and then wham, bam, not even a please and a ring is on your finger."

"I don't want to know that cowboy." Ashni felt grumpy that Sky thought Beck's old-fashioned, grim-jawed acceptance of his fate was somehow gallant. "And I'm not putting a ring on my finger just because I'm pregnant."

Sky nodded. "But it's not just because of the baby. You and Beck love each other. He's crazy about you. And you've been together forever. He's the baby's father. You can't just ignore that."

"I'm not." Ashni felt defensive, which meant Sky was right. But she wasn't ready to admit that. She needed to clutch her armor. Keep her distance.

"I wanted to change my life." She scowled, taking another scoop of the whipped cream. "I should have been more careful about what I asked for."

This was going to be more change than she'd anticipated, and she needed to learn how to live without Beck before the baby came.

"He didn't want to marry me before the baby, so it's not like he really wants to marry me now," she explained. "He just thinks he should. And he made marriage sound like it was no big deal—like we could run down to the courthouse and pay a fee, say I do and that would be that. Marriage means nothing to him. He just wanted to get it over with because now I've become a responsibility."

"Did you tell him how you feel?"

Ashni pressed her lips together, remembering Beck's accusation this week that she hadn't shared her feelings with him—that she'd expected him to read her mind.

"Not exactly." She squirmed. Although she'd piled on the melodrama on her way out the door. She was sure of that even if she couldn't remember her exact words.

"I think you should." Sky sipped her hot chocolate for a beat and then stood up. "I was going to invite you to a fundraising thing we do on the Friday night before the rodeo, but I think you need to talk to Beck. You owe it to him. He's the father. And you owe it to your baby. I don't mean to be harsh, but you got to cowgirl it up, just as I had to when Kane galloped back into my life like a stampeding herd of cattle."

"What do you mean?" Ashni seized on the distraction. She was not ready for Beck to stomp on her heart on the way to the courthouse.

"That, my friend, is a story for another day and another hot chocolate." Sky grinned. "See you tomorrow at the grand unveiling art opening." Sky waved toward the mural. "You rocked this teaching gig. Pure cash. I'd love to talk to you about other ideas for classes."

Ashni nodded eagerly. At least one thing was going right in her life.

"Talk to Beck," Sky reiterated and paused at the door. "And listen."

Chapter Ten

"We did it!" Petal Telford, one of Ashni's youngest but most earnest art students this week, stepped back from the now finished and drying mural. She held her hand up high, shot a selfie with just her eyes, forehead and sleek dark hair poking up in the bottom of the frame. The mural on one wall of the teen room scrolled out in vibrant detail behind her.

"Everyone get in. Sit on the floor." Ashni waved the twelve kids over and climbed up on the top of a stepstool. "I want everyone in the picture. This one is for the Harry's House website and my social media."

The kids clumped together, trying various cool poses. Ashni laughed. She snapped some with her phone but others with a digital camera Beck had bought her last year for Christmas.

"Aren't you going to get a picture of the entire mural?" Petal asked, looking worried.

"Yes, I am." She changed to a wide-angle lens and climbed back up on the stepstool. "You guys slayed it." She paused after taking a couple of shots. "Really spectacular. And that was just in one week. One week," she marveled, shooting a few more frames. "Imagine what you could do if you keep drawing, keep honing your skills."

"Are you going to teach another workshop next year when you come back?" Petal asked.

"Yes. Do. Please." A chorus of voices warmed her heart.

"Actually," she began…and paused. She hadn't told anyone except Sky and Walker Wilder that she was staying on in Marietta—not even her family. She'd worked several hours each day remotely for the rodeo, wrapping up a few projects and handing off others to different staff, and on Monday, she was starting her new job at the public health office that was housed, appropriately, in a small building in the hospital complex.

"Hey, it's your boyfriend," a couple of the girls hollered out. "The cowboy."

A few of the boys whistled under their breath and grinned at her.

Beck leaned against the doorjamb, looking good enough to eat and as if he didn't have a care in the world, whereas her heart seemed engaged in a jumping jack marathon.

"Did you come to see the mural?" Petal asked.

"I did," he said. "I confess I was hoping you'd have an art opening so more of the town could come see it."

"We are," Petal said. "But that's tomorrow morning before the rodeo parade. We're going to meet here with our parents for hot chocolate and muffins because the mural's not dry yet and Ms. Singh still has to paint the frame around the mural, and then tomorrow when we come, we get to sign our painting."

"And someone from the *Courier* is going to come," Lily, Petal's friend, said.

"And also Dylan from the radio station is going to interview us all about the mural and theme," Petal said.

"That's impressive," Beck said. "What's the theme?"

Petal opened her mouth, but Lily slapped her hand over it. "Can you guess?" she dared him.

Beck's eyes widened and he blew out a breath. He sauntered into the classroom to look at the mural more closely. "I can tell right off we got a lot of talented artists in this town," he said. "And a very talented teacher."

He looked at Ash, and she felt as if he was seeing all the way to her soul. His eyes were so warm and his gaze admiring. But he had dark circles under his eyes. Not sleeping. Hurting.

Like me.

Sky's parting words echoed. She'd been afraid to hear Beck out.

Afraid I'll change my mind.

She was doing the right thing though, wasn't she? He could get around her that easily. She loved him that much. So she tried to have everything in place so she couldn't change her mind. But what must that look and feel like to Beck? She'd been so devastated when she'd heard him openly asking Bodhi about what it was like to be with other women. She'd felt betrayed. And rejected, which was what she'd been doing all week to Beck.

Had she been punishing him?

That question didn't sit well at all. But now was not the time to take it out and examine it with a young audience and Beck looking at her with his heart in his eyes.

"You're supposed to be looking at the mural," Ashni reminded him.

"Yes, ma'am," Beck said, still infuriatingly not looking at the mural but at her. "I got a little distracted by another work of art."

The kids responded to that with various noises that had Ashni blushing and Beck's eyes sparkled.

He crossed his arms and rocked back on his heels as he examined each panel of the mural. There was a scene of a farm stand, two kids playing baseball, a mom and two kids baking, a cowboy on a bucking bronc, hat clutched in his hold hand. He took his time, asked the kids who drew which picture and asked them questions—not just about their picture, but about art and what else they liked to do.

Beck was such a natural with everyone, not just kids, although on the tour he always spent the most time with the kids—not as much schmoozing with the corporate sponsors like his cousin Bodhi and a lot of the other cowboys did.

"Seems to me, everything revolves around an aspect of life in Marietta," he said. "I see a lot of the town and the people. Community."

"You got it in one guess." Petal grinned.

"Hey, Miss Ashni, we still going for ice cream?" several of the boys asked.

"Yes. A promise is a promise, and your parents are meeting us at the Scoop to pick you up, but first final cleanup. Just leave the drop cloth."

The kids scrambled, used to the drill. And Beck pitched in. Of course he did. That was one of the things she had always loved about him—how he'd open doors for people, hold them open, pick up something someone had dropped, help friends move, mentor younger cowboys just joining the tour, show up early and stay late at sponsor events, often helping the tour team set up and load up.

She could practically feel her heart goo up, and she wanted to slap herself for weakening so easily. But really, what other choice did she have? He was the father of her child. He wasn't the type of man who would spread out his hands, palms up, and back away and say, "Not mine, no thanks."

They would learn to co-parent. Millions of parents did. That was one of the many reasons she'd taken the job in Marietta. She loved the strong sense of community, of course, but mostly it was because Beck had roots here. He would be back often—perhaps permanently someday—and be able to participate in his child's life.

And when he has another woman by his side?

The snarky question burned as did the jealousy that spread like acid through her veins. For the sake of their child, she vowed she'd be a decent ex.

"Hey now." Beck was behind her as she stood at the sink giving the kids' brushes a final rinse. Only she had the feeling she'd been here for a long time.

She could almost feel the brush of his body against hers—but that was wishful thinking as his hands lightly covered hers while she clutched the brushes under the cold water. Always cold, she'd told the kids, to protect the glue anchoring the bristles.

"I think the bristles are clean." His warm breath teased her cheek.

"Just making sure," she muttered. "Can't be too careful."

She'd always loved Beck's hands—so strong and sure. Callused from so much work, but his fingers were long and blunt at the ends, and he kept his nails neatly trimmed, all the half-moons showing. And his skin was a lighter, golden brown compared to her deeper hue.

His lips briefly touch the curl of her ear. "Yes, baby, you can." His hands closed more fully over hers, and he gave her a light, reassuring squeeze.

She closed her eyes and willed her body to stop trembling.

Beck reached around and turned off the water and spread the brushes out on the soft cloth she'd laid out so that they would dry.

She felt a little bit like she was coming out of a spell when she turned around and saw him watching her so intently. His eyes looked darker, his cheeks hollower, and the Copper-Mountain-high planes of his cheeks looked even starker than usual.

But his scrutiny warmed as she stared at him helplessly.

"It's going to be okay, Ash," he whispered. "Better than

okay."

She could barely breathe, much less swallow all of the tension clawing at her suddenly. She didn't see how he could say that. It was wishful thinking, and she'd been doing too much wishing and dreaming for the both of them. She had to be strong.

Gulping in a shaky breath, she quickly—and cowardly—walked toward the students grouped eagerly around the door.

"Ice cream!" She pasted on a happy, look-how-unaffected-I-am smile and rushed out of Harry's House. Hopefully, she could calm herself enough to act normal by the time they arrived at the ice cream parlor.

No such luck. Just as she was registering that the warm, late-September afternoon had turned breezy with a definite chill now that the sun was beginning to set, Beck draped her denim jacket over her shoulders.

"Thank you," she murmured, keeping her attention on the group of pre and young teens walking with them.

She would not look into his beautiful eyes. She would not let her gaze linger on his lips that knew how to kiss her senseless and drive her over the edge again and again. She could resist Beck. She just needed to practice. But darn the man, he made it near impossible when she could smell his cedar, citrus and spice scent. He walked so close to her, reminding her how it felt to belong.

Ignore him.

Hard to do when they arrived at the ice cream store.

Beck insisted on treating, and when she demurred, he shot her a wicked smile and ordered her favorite, pistachio, and his, peanut butter and chocolate, in one cone.

"Milk," he whispered in her ear. "It does a body or two bodies good."

His breath was warm, his lips cold from the lick he'd stolen, and he held out the cone for her to take a swipe.

She was supposed to say "no thank you," but she was so undone by his nearness and his casual reference to the baby that she could only stare up at him.

"You love ice cream." His tender sky-blue gaze warmed with heat, and as she continued to stare at him, transfixed like an idiot, his gaze darkened.

"Take a picture and put it on your screen saver," Declan, probably one of the best cartoonists in the entire class, urged. "You two are blocking the line."

Ashni took a quick step back, but Beck followed and casually looped his arm around her waist. He held the cone closer to her lips, and Ashni gave up. She told herself it was to avoid creating any more attention—especially as several parents were starting to arrive—but really it was because she felt herself starting to crack. It felt so good to be held. She'd been making so many changes so quickly and then learning about the baby had been disorienting. Beck seemed so steady. Her rock.

These four days without Beck had been wonderful in some ways and achingly lonely in others. She'd had so many new experiences, and yet he hadn't been there to share any of them with her.

Because you shut him out.

She felt guilty and confused—as if she were keeping secrets from him, the one person she'd never lied to or had held back any part of herself.

Until recently.

Trust her conscience—nudged by Sky—to not just niggle but to shout. Ashni angled her head and placed her hand lightly over his to bring the cone closer so she could have a taste of pistachio.

She closed her eyes and stifled a groan. She loved pistachio ice cream. LOVED it. And she often denied herself because she tried her best to avoid sugar in her diet for health reasons.

"I like the way we usually eat it," Beck said softly.

In bed.

Of course he'd remind her of that now, here, in public with her students laughing and talking and greeting their parents and enthusing about the day. Ashni nearly choked on her second lick of ice cream.

"I've missed you," Beck said, pain in his eyes, but then he smiled at the gathering groups of parents and students. "Showtime," he said, echoing what she often said before one of his rodeo events or sponsor-driven appearances started.

Ashni greeted the parents, reminded them of the official unveiling tomorrow morning before the start of the parade. She was surprised at how quickly everyone left, leaving her alone with Beck.

He had stood a little distance off while she'd said goodbye to everyone, but now he was close—clearly trying to assess her mood, much like she'd seen him do with horses or bulls over the years. The thought made her smile. Maybe people weren't so far up the evolutionary ladder as they thought.

"I've missed your smile," he said. "I've missed you. I miss us."

Ashni wasn't sure what to say. How to look him in the eye and tell him about all the changes she'd set in motion, but she needed to do that—be fair. Be clear. She didn't feel ready. It would feel too much like goodbye.

But that's what you wanted.

Always the voice questioning her every move. She did want to stand on her own. But maybe it was more to prove that she could rather than wanting to be without Beck.

They shared a child.

The knowledge thrilled and terrified.

"Let's take a walk." She could barely force the words through her suddenly dry throat and mouth.

She could feel herself tremble as she laced her fingers with his.

This was the next step. Where would it lead?

HOLDING HANDS WAS a simple thing, and yet Beck felt such pleasure as they walked across Court Street toward the courthouse. Crews strung lights through the trees in the park and set up the temporary concert stage and dance floor for the Saturday night steak dinner—a fundraiser for the Montana Cattlemen's Association that was always followed by a concert with several live bands and a dance.

He didn't want to break the fragile peace between then, but he burned to ask Ash what her plans were now that the class was over—if she'd watch him compete or be his guest at the steak dinner and dance with him under the stars. He'd never had to ask before. She'd always attended social events with him. Bodhi and Bowen had always had to find dates.

My turn to do the wooing.

He watched Ash carefully lick, avoiding the peanut butter and chocolate to get to the pistachio ice cream—the delicate flicks of her tongue fascinated him.

She hummed a little as she licked.

"Ice cream seems to stay down."

"Have you been nauseous?" he asked, worried. Ash was already so petite and athletically slim. She couldn't afford to lose much weight in her first trimester, which he'd read sometimes happened in one of the pregnancy books he'd downloaded last night when once again he hadn't been able to sleep. If he and Ash didn't get straight, he'd probably coma out by the first rodeo event.

"Pretty much," she said. "But not unbearable."

"That's good," he said, mentally reminding himself to research healthy foods that would be easy for her to keep down. "A walk in the park?" he asked lightly, bracing himself for her to brush him off like she'd done all week.

"I would have thought you'd want to go by the fairgrounds."

Normally he would. To check on his horses and to get a feel for the space. Visualize his rides, his events. But not tonight.

"Let's do something different. What do you want to do?"

"Whatever you want."

"No." He turned and faced her. "That's just it. You often agree or defer, and that ultimately made you unhappy, and I didn't realize because you didn't tell me. So, you need to tell me what you're feeling. And what you want and what you need."

Her expression clouded.

This was so hard when everything with Ash had been so easy. Now he understood what the expression "walking through a minefield" meant.

"Let's walk in the park," she said softly, "then maybe by the river."

"Sounds good."

He thought of things to say but rejected them. Too fraught or too accusatory. He felt like he'd been running on adrenaline all week and was about to crash. He wanted to avoid any of the places Bodhi might go tonight. If Bodhi saw them together, he'd probably joke with Ash about the dumb Rodeo Bride Game and how he'd be disqualified for roping Ash into it. He didn't need any more outside interference with everything so tenuous with Ash. He was leaving his cousins to it. Building his future with Ash was too precious and felt precarious.

Yesterday he'd caught Bodhi and Nico kissing on some hay bales they were supposed to be setting up for seats for the guests during the Ballantyne Bash. She'd had Bodhi's shirt untucked and her hands had been walking all over him—nothing really new there, Bodhi had hardly lived a monk's life and excelled in PDA, except this time he'd stepped in front to hide Nico's state of undress, which Beck already had been trying to mentally unsee. Then he'd ordered him in a harsh voice to get lost. Bodhi had never minded getting caught. Ever.

Beck breathed in the night. He'd faced bucking bulls, bucking broncs with and without saddles. He could wrestle a steer to the ground faster than most cowboys. He was known to excel during clutch moments, and he had no intention of screwing up the most important moment in his life.

At least Ashni still held his hand, not actively, but she wasn't pulling away, and he'd store that in his win column for now.

"Do you think you'd like to teach more art classes to kids?"

He was already picturing her having some hands-on art activities for kids at the rodeo meet and greets as the rodeo season wound down. Lots of sponsors and VIPs brought their families. Or when they settled in Marietta—if they settled in Marietta—she could teach at Harry's House.

"Yes. I would like that. It felt good to be creative, to be

part of something. I had dinner at Sky's one night, and she showed me her studio and we talked about art so late that I ended up spending the night. It was like college again—having a friend and making plans."

Her voice rang with enthusiasm. Alarm skittered through him, but he forced it away. This was important. He'd asked her to tell him what she needed. It was his job to listen. Not react. But he felt like she was still flowing further downstream away from him.

They walked through the park, stood by the river and listened to the water burble. He wrapped his arms around her and pulled her back to his chest. It felt so good to hold her. She sighed, and he closed his eyes, just letting the feel of her, the warmth of her settle into his skin.

He finally broke the silence. "Ash, I want to talk about the baby."

I want to talk about us.

She made a little sound, and for the first time in what felt like forever, her beautiful, liquid-black eyes met his searching gaze.

"I got in to see a doctor today." She stunned him. "I'm nine weeks pregnant. Everything looks good. I heard the heartbeat." Her palm drifted over her still-flat stomach. "I'm an us," she whispered.

Beck felt like she'd stabbed him.

His first impulse was to lay claim, and he barely bit back the words. His emotions rioted inside of him like a bucking bronc out of the chute, only he didn't have his center of gravity, and he was going to be thrown.

"Beck?"

He didn't trust himself to speak. She was cutting him out of her life and their child's life. And she expected him to just suck it up.

"Beck?" She turned around in his arms, which had loosened.

"You're happy about the baby," he stated.

This time it was he who avoided eye contract. Instead he stared at the reeds that marked the river's path farther downstream—lit by the glow of the lights in the park and the rising moon—trying to calm down. Not react.

She didn't want him.

She didn't trust him.

She didn't respect him.

"Yes," she said softly, wonderingly. "I am. I was shocked. I always wanted to be a mom. I know we weren't planning on a baby but…"

"So now we *are* a we? Am I in or out in your new plan? Would you just prefer I get back on the road and out of your life forever?"

"I…Beck—" She broke off. "You're angry."

"Hell yeah. Angry doesn't begin to cover it. But since I'm trying to not let this be about me, and you clearly don't want anything to be about me anymore, please enlighten me about what I did that was so terrible that you would not want me to be a part of our child's life?"

Her eyes filled with tears.

He did his best to ignore them. She kept shoving him away. The hurt and frustration from the past week ripped out of him, and he didn't want to hold back anymore.

"Yes, I said something stupid to my cousin one time a month or two ago. I didn't act on the question. I'd never act on it because I love you, and I don't want another woman ever. And yet for you, voicing one question is such a crime that I must be cut out of my child's life."

"I...well, not cut out entirely." For the first time Beck could remember, Ashni struggled for words.

Fine. Because he had plenty.

"That's generous. What about your role in the F-up?"

"Me?"

"Yeah. What you should have done, if you were pissed about something I said, was get in my face and demand an explanation, not run away and nurse a wound that infects and festers without ever letting me know what's wrong. I know I hurt you, Ash, and I am sorry, but you've got to give me something to work with. You have to tell when you're pissed. Or when you're hurt. You have to tell me when you're bored or unhappy. You have to tell me what you want. You have to share your dreams with me. That's what couples do. Communicate."

Her tears flowed freely now and he brushed at them carefully with his thumbs.

"I can't be your man if you don't tell me what you want or feel."

She burrowed into him, and he held her. His heart

slammed as hard as hers, and his breath came in tight gasps, but for the moment, he finally felt like he was on solid ground.

"I'm sorry I didn't talk to you about re-upping on the tour." He kissed the top of her head and then down her silky hair. Her arms were around him now, squeezing with strength that always surprised him since she was petite. "I'd been toying with the idea of when to quit the tour, checking in with my investment broker, trying to figure out how much was enough money."

She rocked back and looked up at him. "I didn't know that."

"We always talked about settling in Marietta." He watched her carefully, relieved when she nodded. "So I've been exploring other career options—stock contracting. Breeding bulls or bucking broncs. The cattle ranch can't support all of us once we have families. We've always known we'd have to branch the business out."

Ash focused on him intently—her luminous gaze like a Montana starry sky.

"But something happened to Bodhi. He changed after his birthday, and I'd been worried about him since the end of last season. He's been off. Reckless. Mean. In my face. He's taking chances, picking the rankest bulls and the rankest broncs. It's like he's trying to get hurt. And then he's been almost compulsive, picking up women. I just feel like he's this close to being out of control."

"Oh, Beck," she said. "You didn't tell me."

"He was cutting himself off, and I didn't want him to be alone. And I didn't want the burden to fall on Bowen. And Bowen's more shut down. He hardly talks to me anymore. Doesn't want to hang out."

"I didn't see it." Ash sounded remorseful.

"Not your fault, baby. You and Bodhi are such friends. You share the love of science and are always discussing research articles and discoveries. He's calmer with you. That night I thought if I talked to him, made him see how empty his life was, how he was burning himself out, running too hot, too fast, too…I thought I could make him see that he was limiting himself to just physical relationships and that he should slow down. Find someone. He deserves to be loved like I was loved."

Her breaths came in little puffs, then she reached up and cupped his face. He turned his cheek into her palm.

"I thought you were bored with me," she admitted in a pained whisper.

"What?" The idea was so out there he couldn't even take it seriously. "No. Never. Of course not. I saw you that day through the window in the musical theater room in high school and heard you sing, and it was like being jolted to life. I was done. I'd found my person. I've never once not felt like you are my one."

"Beck," she whispered, fingers trembling. He turned his head and pressed his lips to her palm, savoring the warmth and texture of her skin. Then she did the most incredible thing. She took his hand and brought it down to cover her abdomen. And for Beck, who'd had a difficult year and an awful week, and who knew he and Ash still had so much to hash out, he suddenly felt the connection. Everything felt right and once again, he was on solid ground.

Chapter Eleven

Walking down Main Street with Beck felt right. She'd held him at such a distance all week and hadn't realized the toll it had taken. She also had to admit that she'd shoved all the blame on Beck for letting their lives and their relationship drift, but during this week she'd gained perspective and saw how she too had played an equal if not bigger role in their problems.

There was still so much to tell him. So much they had to discuss—and the sonogram picture to show him, but she felt like she could finally breathe. They could talk later. Now she just wanted to be Ash and Beck, together.

She held Beck's hand, and their bodies kept brushing up each other, like they often did as if magnetically charged. She leaned her head against his arm and just breathed him in, savoring his familiar scent and warmth.

Many of the shops were still open, and the street still had quite a lot of foot traffic. Beck stopped in front of Sage's chocolate shop.

"Let's get one of your favorite treats," he suggested.

She almost admitted that by far he was her favorite treat, but that would be like pulling a pin on a grenade, and Beck would hustle her back to her room. Part of her ached for that conclusion to the evening, yet another part still needed to hold back, protect herself. She was exhausted but until she was confident she'd hold strong and not fall back into old patterns of not discussing her feelings and wants, she didn't want to jump back in bed. She needed to also support his dreams the way she wanted him to support hers. No more deferring to someday, or a vague timeline she didn't help control.

Beck heading back out on tour would give her some time to think and gain confidence in her new direction and to come to terms with an unexpected pregnancy.

Beck cradled her hand in his and kissed each one of her knuckles, then her wrist. The soft brush of his lips and the warmth of his exhaled breath sent shivers darting through her.

"Beck, don't seduce me," she whispered.

Even she heard the "yet" in there.

"I think that's your fault," he said hoarsely. "I can't help myself when I'm with you. I need to hold you. I want to be inside you."

She stared up at him, mutely, unable to resist, even knowing she should.

The kiss started so sweetly—just a brush of lips, but then Ashni felt as if he'd struck a match on her skin. She leaned into Beck, and her hands clutched the fabric of his black-and-white western-style shirt.

"Ash." His voice ached, and then he smiled ruefully.

"Trying to be a gentleman here, and you, my beautiful girl, are not helping."

He held her close for a moment, and she could feel the strength of his body, the hard press of his sex, which blasted heat straight through her.

"Behave," he whispered.

"You first."

He straightened up and laughed. "Not sure that's going to happen, but I'll give it my best shot."

They entered the store and the scent of Sage's famous hot chocolate permeated the room, nearly drugging in its deliciousness. She and Beck looked over the chocolate selection. He watched her closely as if trying to suss out what she wanted before even she knew.

She loved it all. She chose the individually wrapped chocolate cowboy boots, one for each of her students, and then some dark chocolate salted caramels—her favorite and also a few nut clusters to share with Beck. He, of course, insisted on paying for it all and included a box of mixed chocolate truffles for his mom and one for both of his aunts and a box of assorted chocolates for his granddad. He added a hot chocolate for them to split on top of it all.

"We're buying so much, Sage," Ashni said as Sage's niece, Portia, put bows on each of the copper-colored boxes. "You'll have to get up early for tomorrow when the crowds really descend."

"Oh, they've descended." Sage laughed and pushed her coppery-colored hair away from her face with her arm. "I've been coming in early and staying late all week to prepare, but it's my passion, and I've got a good crew." She smiled fondly at her niece. "Whipped cream?" she asked as she poured out the chocolate that simmered in a copper pot.

"That's the best part," Beck said.

Sage added a towering dollop, and Beck's eyes widened. He reached for the hot chocolate, but Sage shook her head with mock disapproval and handed it to Ashni.

"Manners, cowboy," she admonished.

Beck carried the bag of chocolates while Ash cradled the hot chocolate in her palms.

They walked out of the store. The evening was a little brisk, but Ashni wasn't ready to call an end.

"Cold?" Beck was already sliding his denim jacket off and draping it around her shoulders.

"A little, thanks." She smiled. He'd always been attentive, often noticing how she felt or what she needed before she did.

She took a sip of the hot chocolate. The flavors danced over her tongue. Whipped cream was on the tip of her nose. Beck swooped in and kissed it off. Then his lips settled firmly over hers, persuading them apart. Ashni sighed and melted into him and his kiss.

"Sage must be responsible for many romances," he murmured, kissing his way down her neck and igniting a whole different set of shivers.

"Your turn," she said breathlessly holding out the drink to him.

"You keep it," he encouraged. "I intend to take full advantage of any future whipped cream malfunctions."

He smiled, but worry still squatted in his gaze.

From the moment she'd seen the positive pregnancy test, she'd bravely told herself she could raise a child on her own, and she could, but tonight she admitted to herself she didn't want to.

But she didn't want to marry Beck because of the baby.

And she had no idea how to move forward.

"Beck, I don't know what to do."

She heard the fear in her voice and hated it. She wanted to be strong. Independent.

"Let's just enjoy the night," Beck said. "Together."

"It's not that easy," she said seeing all the obstacles ahead, but Beck was Beck. In the moment. One problem at a time. One event. Then the next. Total focus.

BECK FELT LIKE he could breathe again as they continued to walk down Main Street. He no longer felt like he was sitting on an unexploded bomb, and yet he sensed Ashni was holding something back. But then, so was he.

But he wanted to savor this moment of peace, and hopefully it would keep him from doing something stupid like marching her to the courthouse first thing Monday morning. Or buying her a gigantic ring tonight.

His steps slowed outside the jewelry store.

"Beck." Ashni's voice was a whisper of sound, but he knew what she meant. He squashed down the disappointment. Too much. Too soon. But it felt too late.

"But I want to buy you something," he insisted. Of course he pushed. It was the Ballantyne way. "A celebration of the baby."

"The baby we spent years trying not to have?" Her jaw angled in challenge.

"Don't say that," he said urgently. "Every child should be welcome. Our child will be loved and very welcomed."

He couldn't wait to tell his family. But he wanted to tell all of them together with Ash. At the Ballantyne Bash. His cousins could play their game, and his granddad might still head to Denver, but he and Ash and their child were real, enduring. His.

"Our child will be," she said firmly. She looked into the store. "Okay, something for the baby. No ring."

"Yet."

Her lips firmed, and the softness of her gaze hardened.

"Ash, I want to spend my life with you. You know that."

She crossed her arms. "You always changed the subject when I brought up marriage."

"You didn't exactly bring it up," he pointed out, even as guilt pricked. She'd hinted, and by the deeply skeptical look she leveled at him, he was busted. "I love you too much to lose you."

"Huh?"

He felt like the biggest idiot standing outside a jewelry

store with a sidewalk sale on western-style charm bracelets and belt buckles and other assorted rodeo-themed ware priced to sell, and about to spill his guts.

"I watched my mom get married and divorced four times. Four."

Ash had been there for the last one, which had lasted less time than the one before. "I hated it. I hated her for being so stupid and the men for being so wrong. I didn't want that for you and me."

Ashni sighed. "I know," she said. "But you never talked about it, and I guess I took my cue from you. I didn't think that would happen to us. You always seemed so invincible. Confident."

He'd never shared his doubts with her.

And she hadn't told him her concerns.

And they needed to do better. Starting now.

"You were always my safe place," he admitted like the biggest knuckleheaded cowboy. If Bodhi could see him now, he'd never stop laughing. "You're magic. I didn't want to ruin that," he admitted. "And I wanted you to think…" Oh. God. This was hard. "That I could handle anything. Be your hero."

Ashni swallowed hard and blinked a few times. Damn. He'd made her cry again. "We need to handle joys and problems together," she said softly.

He nodded too choked up to speak.

"Pick something special for the baby, Beck." She propelled him inside the store and then walked a little way down the street and stared up at the moon.

Feeling undone, Beck entered the store and tried to pull himself together. He'd been in a lot of jewelry stores over the years. But this time, it was a big deal.

He walked straight to the engagement rings. When he'd researched online, he'd familiarized himself with what he should be looking for and designs he thought Ash would like. He didn't want to rush his choice, so he made an appointment for tomorrow—rodeos were pretty consuming, but he wanted to find Ash a ring to make his intentions clear to her, his family and hers.

He wanted a round-cut diamond in a filigree or antique setting, and the assistant said she would pull together a selection for him to look at tomorrow morning. She even agreed to meet him early, before the store opened.

Then she showed him a few necklaces with Montana sapphires—his favorite stone—and he immediately saw the one he wanted: a delicate half of a gold heart connected to another half of a gold heart by a teal Montana sapphire at the bottom of the higher heart. Each side would remain forever connected yet asymmetrical.

"Unusual," he murmured, feeling like his hands were so large compared to the delicately wrought piece. "And beautiful."

"We have a new jewelry designer we are contracting with. This was the first necklace she brought to us. It's fairly expensive," the assistant said apologetically. "She's gaining quite a following and takes commissions within many price ranges. I can give you her card."

"Yes, please, and the necklace. I don't need it wrapped."

Beck dangled the necklace from his finger and went outside. Ashni nibbled on a chocolate boot and still stared up at the sky. He smiled. She'd always loved to do that. Often he'd drive them out of whatever town they were staying in and they'd spread out blankets in the back of his rig and stargaze.

"Close your eyes," he invited.

She did. He carefully fastened the unusual clasp the assistant had had to demonstrate twice.

"Open."

Ashni smiled. "Thank you." She felt the precious metal, the stone. "Cool shape," she said and pulled her phone out of her pocket so she could see the necklace. "Beck, it's so beautiful. I love it. But it looks expensive." She worried her bottom lip with her teeth.

"You're not supposed to worry about that," he reminded her.

"It's really unique. Gorgeous." Her fingers skimmed over the design.

He often bought her jewelry—earrings, necklaces—to create memories. Usually she preferred shorter chains so the medallion or stone would lay just below her clavicles. This chain was longer, and he liked that the lower heart nestled closer to the valley between her breasts.

It was elegant and sexy as hell. Longing and desire rose up so fast and fierce. He didn't know how to contain that much emotion, that much want.

"I know I've been pushy most of this week even as I tried to give you space. And we still have a lot to talk about. I know all that, and we talked about being more communicative with each other and honest about our needs," he said in a rush. "And, Ash, I really, want to be alone with you. I need to hold you."

SEXUAL DESIRE AND emotions were strange and wild and wicked beasts, Ash mused as she and Beck cut down several streets and back toward her apartment. Was she making a mistake? Probably. But it was hers to make. And tonight, it didn't feel like a mistake.

"Beck, I want to be fair." She stopped at the base of her stairs. "My emotions are all over the place. I have a lot going on here—" she touched her head "—and here—" she touched her heart. "I don't know the next step for us." She placed her hands on his chest. He was so firm. His heartbeat steady. Strong.

"We are having a child. That will forever link us, but…" she paused "…if I invite you up, it doesn't mean things are going to go back to normal," she cautioned. "That string is cut. I love you. I always have. But this is not the yes you probably want…the yes we are a couple again. The yes to living together or marrying."

"But it's a maybe." Lust and challenge stamped his features, lit his heated blue gaze so that they sparkled like gems.

"An open door."

Statement. Not a question. So Beck. Seize the challenge. Declare victory.

"I don't know," she admitted.

Beck's answering smile was hungry, and Ash felt like he'd already ripped off her clothes, pillaged her mouth and plunged deep inside her as her body liquefied under the heat of his gaze.

"Give me the key, Ash. I'll unlock the door. Take my chances."

ASHNI PULLED OUT a key attached to a blinged-out cowgirl boot, and something inside him snapped. He swooped her up in his arms and ran up the stairs. Her gold sandals fell off, first one then the other.

He unlocked the door, didn't bother with the lights because the party lights strung up around the patio bathed the room in a gold glow.

He put her back on her feet. His denim jacket slid off her shoulders and hit the floor, and he eased off hers, and laid it on the sofa.

"You said you went to the doctor." His voice sounded like he'd swallowed gravel. It still hurt that she'd gone without him. His fingers played with the strap of her sundress. Only a bow held it up on each delicate shoulder. He wondered if she was wearing a bra.

"Yes," she said and hesitated.

"Is it safe for us to...you know?"

Ashni removed his hat and set it carefully on the head of the plush artistic horse that dominated her sofa.

She reached into her cross-body purse and pulled out a square black-and-white photo that she held to her chest.

"Beck, I should have waited for you to see the doctor. I know that. But I was hurt and angry and confused. Everything seemed to be hitting me at once, and I just wanted some peace and space to sort it out. Our life has been so loud with the constant travel, the rush of working in the PR marketing machine of the tour, arranging so many small events with local hospitals, and organizations and sponsors, and then your day-to-day life with competing and the injuries and the worry, and your cousins always underfoot. I never had quiet time to reflect and didn't realize how much I needed time and quiet."

"I wish—" He stopped. Of course he wished she'd told him. But what would he have done? The end of the season was always a grind. Chasing money, a position in the finals. The pressure cranked. Nagging pain and injuries accelerated. The physical, mental and emotional toll was tremendous and often knocked cowboys out of the finals and money in the last few weeks.

Don't make excuses. Let her talk.

He could practically hear Bowen's voice in his head, counseling him. Bowen had always been the one he'd turned to when he'd had a problem, never his mom. She would criticize, take over, tell him all the things he'd done wrong, generalize his incompetence, blame him and then fix it—never letting him forget she knew better.

So he'd shut her out. Hid most of his life from her.

Like Ash started doing.

"We'll communicate better," he vowed. They couldn't go back, but he could be a better partner going forward.

"I have a picture of the baby," she said shyly. "I got a couple so you could have one. I know I shut you out, and I'm sorry," she said in a rush. "But—"

"Show me," he offered. He could do this. Leave the hurt of the past week where it belonged—in the past.

Ash handed the square black-and-white photo to him.

Beck stared, unable to believe what he was seeing. He'd thought it would look more…he didn't even know. Blobbish. But he could see a head and a body, and was that an arm?

"Everything looks normal. The organs are forming, and even teeth under the gums," she said in awe. "The baby is about the size of a strawberry."

"We're having a baby," he said.

"I know."

He stared at the picture a little longer and then pulled out his phone and took a photo. He didn't want to hide the news from his family. Not anymore. His cousins were going to be uncles—not technically, but that would be the reality of the role they'd play in his child's life.

And his mom would be a grandma.

How would she take that?

And Granddad. He'd be a great-granddad. What would their baby call him? Would he feel less alone when he and Ash told him that they were expecting and wanting to settle at Three Tree Ranch?

"I can hear you thinking," Ash said.

Beck kissed the picture and then put it on the table. His eyes pricked hot, and he blinked several times to try to clear them.

Ash slid her arms around him. For a moment, peace and happiness drifted through him, and then Ash's fingers played with the snaps of his shirt.

He'd been semi-hard all night, and all the blood in his body seemed to rush south, further taunting his control.

"Ashni, are you sure?" He faced her.

"I don't want to think any more tonight." She pulled on her dress's bows on her shoulders. The shift-style dress puddled at her feet, leaving her only in pink panties and a bandeau-style matching bra.

Thinking was definitely overrated. Beck pounced.

HE EVEN GROWLED, which woke a primitive side of her that only Beck had ever unleashed. He made her feel powerful and sexy and alive. He tugged her bra off with his teeth and laved one peaked nipple with his tongue and sucked it into the heat of his mouth, while his fingers expertly toyed with her other breast. Ashni groaned her pleasure. Her breasts were so sensitive now, almost to the point of pain, but the bite of pain merged spectacularly with pleasure and she swore she saw pinpricks of light.

"You have too many clothes on." She pulled frantically at the snaps on his shirt. How was it she was only in panties and Beck was fully clothed? That had to be some sort of crime.

"Where the hell is the bed?"

He'd picked her up, and she wrapped her legs around his lean hips, loving how his erection pressed hard against her soaked heat.

"You've been creative without a bed before." She clung to his hewn shoulders and arched her back so that he'd kiss and suck on her aching nipples.

He swore under his breath, and Ashni felt the cork stoppering her aching misery pop. She felt free and laughed even as she rode desperation's knife edge.

"Hurry," she urged breathlessly, trying to reach in between their bodies so that she could work off his belt buckle, kissing his mouth and nipping on his lip. His hiss of air cranked her higher.

She loved Beck fast and urgent and a little crazy for her, but she wanted to feel all of him—needed to after the time apart and all of her uncertainty. "Handle," she murmured against his mouth even as she reached down and managed to undo his rodeo buckles. His Wranglers' button took even less work.

"Huh?"

"Bed. Handle. Pull." She had her hands in his hair now, yanking his head right where she needed it. "Yes," she cried as his lips tightened over her nipple and his tongue and teeth teased it. She was so close. So close. And Beck had barely started.

She'd never been with another man, but she couldn't imagine anyone In. The. World better in bed or out than Beck.

He understood her moaned commands and pulled the bed down and she was immediately flat on it, bra and panties over her hips and on the floor and then Beck's body was between her thighs.

He kicked off his boots and shucked off his jeans.

"Inside me." She tried to haul him up her body. And why did he still have boxers on? She caught them with her toes and tugged down. "Now."

He laughed and pulled them off. He stared at her glistening core like it was something new.

"Dessert first."

"Beck," she protested and agreed at the same time and then his shoulders wedged her wider, making her feel excited and exposed and vulnerable all at once. His tongue slid between her plump, wet folds, and she forgot how to speak. Her orgasm hit shockingly fast, but Beck didn't stop. He continued to alternate licking and sucking on her clit with stroking her with his thumb while he crisscrossed his fingers deep inside her. Her second orgasm took longer, but hit stronger, and she seemed to float on top of the wave endlessly.

She settled back into her body, with Beck kissing his way leisurely back up to her neck while she trembled and panted beneath him. She tried to urge him where she wanted him, but she lacked strength and coordination and apparently speech.

"I love you," Beck murmured between drugging kisses. "I've missed you."

Me too.

But she only stared at him, curious as to what he would do next.

He braced himself on his elbows and stared at her so intensely she felt as if his body and soul merged with hers.

Soul mates. She felt like she was standing on a precipice.

He'd been so passionate moments before, but when he slowly began to inch into her body, holding her gaze as surely as he held her heart, Ashni felt as if this were their first time all over again.

Chapter Twelve

BECK WALKED THROUGH a maze of trucks and rigs toward the back entrance of the fairgrounds. The late sun warmed his shoulders. The familiarity of the scene—cowboys preparing for their first event, jawing with each other, some even flirting with the rodeo queens who were already mounted, silk flags unfurled but still by their sides and their hair artfully curled—filled him with a sense of rightness.

Copper Mountain Rodeo.

Marietta, Montana.

Home.

And after his night and dawn with Ashni, all felt right with his world.

He should be tired. It wasn't like they'd slept much last night, and they'd both been up early—lots to do. But he felt invigorated. He had an afternoon of competition, and then the steak dinner. There would be good eats—his granddad was one of the beef suppliers each year—and great music and dancing with Ashni under the stars.

And tonight he was going to propose. Not wait until the Bash. Not try to make it showy or public. His proposal was real, not like the Rodeo Bride Game pretend public marriage proposals. He and Ash were the real deal, forever, not a game to persuade Granddad to stay put on his beloved ranch. Beck would use his brain and his business proposal he'd been piecing together over the past couple of years. And now Boone Telford had added another idea to his mix.

No matter what, he and Ash would work.

And tomorrow, before the Ballantyne Bash, when his family was all together, he and Ashni would announce their big news.

A baby. Marriage.

He wished the marriage had come before the baby. Then Ashni wouldn't have to doubt his intentions—although the baby had made marriage more imminent, not some fuzzy, distant mirage he avoided because he didn't want to walk the same road his mom had.

He'd been dumb to wait so long—wanting closure on his rodeo life first and letting his mom's marriages weigh him down.

But that was the past. Today was a new start. And tomorrow, he was going to win at least a couple of his events and take her to the Ballantyne Bash as his fiancée. He was feeling so positive, he'd even looked online at some dogs available for adoption at a local shelter in Marietta and another in Livingston. Ash could pick their dog, and they could pick it up after the tour finished this year.

He reached the stall where he kept Raider and Gallatin. The two horses, who'd had their heads together as if communicating, turned toward him.

"Good morning again, beautiful," he murmured, first to Raider and then to Gallatin as he aggressively leaned into Beck's shoulder for attention. "Yes, of course you too." He smiled, too caught up in the moment to care about the other cowboys readying their horses for steer wrestling.

"I see how it is." Ashni's voice burbled with laughter behind him. "You're very generous handing out the B compliments today."

Beck laughed. He had woken her by calling her beautiful before making slow love to her and then he'd walked her to Harry's House so that she could paint the frame for the mural. Then he'd taken care of his horses, checked in with his grandfather to see what the plan was for today before heading to Harry's House and greeted her with "beautiful," again shortly before the students and parents started arriving for the opening of the mural.

He'd been pleased for Ashni that so many people had shown up—members of the Harry's House board of directors, families and also community members. He'd had had his first breathless wonder moment not about the baby but about the baby becoming a kid with likes and dislikes and talents or struggles. What would their child want to do—art? Sports? Rodeo? Dance? Design computer games?

"Yours was beautiful with a capital B," he defended, kissing her cheek. His granddad was with her, and he looked happy and robust and normal. It was like the sun had finally emerged.

"Pretty neat save," she acknowledged.

"I said it more than once today, and I'll say it again. You are beautiful," he said, taking in her petite frame, still hiding their news. Her hair was in waves and loosely held in a side ponytail with a turquoise clasp.

Ash often wore simple-cut dresses or sundresses that showcased her toned, feminine frame, but today she had opted for a trim, dark denim pantsuit with shiny copper buttons. She'd left one button more than usual undone so he could catch a little shadowy cleavage at some angles, and yes, he was looking. He also saw the glint of the new necklace, and considering what she hopefully would be wearing later today, excitement skittered down his spine.

"You look amazing," he said.

Ash laughed. "You say that whatever I wear." She smiled at Ben Ballantyne. "Look at him with the compliments." She squeezed his granddad's arm, who smiled indulgently. "I think he got his charm from you."

"Not saying." Ben Ballantyne joined in the teasing. "It could have been Bodhi. That boy could charm a prairie rattlesnake out of its skin since he could talk."

"Bodhi does seem to be popular wherever he goes," Ash admitted. "Although today, I saw him making the rounds at the parade with an auburn-haired beauty, and he was looking particularly smitten. And—" she dropped her voice to a stage whisper "—it was the same woman I saw him with on Sunday night nearly a week ago at Grey's. A record."

"Definitely not saying." Ben's lips twitched.

"You don't have to," Ashni sassed. "Beck, I walked with your granddad from the Java Café to the fairgrounds. I think every woman young, old and in between in Marietta knows his name and has something to say, and everyone is especially excited about the Ballantyne Bash this year."

"That they did." Ben Ballantyne smiled and his still-sharp blue eyes sparkled.

Not for the first time did Beck wonder why his granddad had never remarried. His wife had died while she'd been training a new horse for barrel racing a few years before Beck had been born. Mom had been just out of college.

"He has a special announcement at the Bash, apparently," Ash said. "But it's top secret. He won't even tell me." She zipped her lips.

"All my boys are full of schemes," his granddad said. "And so am I."

"What?" Beck felt a jolt, but Granddad looked innocent, almost suspiciously so. No. He couldn't suspect anything. Besides, he and Ashni had nothing to hide.

"We won't keep you." She kissed his cheek. "Just wanted to wish you good luck today. We'll be cheering for you."

"She really just wanted to show off her new boots," his granddad teased.

Beck had been too busy noticing how beautiful Ash was and how happy she looked. She glowed and the denim pantsuit clung to her very fit, feminine body. He dragged his gaze obediently lower.

"Sweet. I got myself a designer cowgirl," he said.

"Now you just need to hang on to her." His granddad slipped his arm through Ashni's. "See if your skills wrestling steers into submission and keeping your head and your seat on a bucking bronc translate to success out of the arena."

He led Ash away while Beck watched, more than a bit shocked that his granddad had all but dissed him. At least Ash did look back, smile and wave.

"You gonna keep watching your girl walk away?" Bodhi joined him, leading Cash, one of the best horses he and Bodhi had ever trained. "Or are you actually back in the game?"

That damn game.

"That game is going to bite one of us in the ass," Beck complained. "Besides, Ash is not a game."

"Life's a game, all of it. Play or you're cut from the lineup."

Bodhi's blue eyes shone bright. He seemed keyed up. A different energy jangled through him, putting Beck on edge.

"Jesus, what did you have for breakfast? In the Buddhaholistically brilliant words of Taylor Swift, you need to calm down."

"I will when I'm dead."

"I thought Bowen was my hazer today."

"Then you drew the short straw," Bodhi said. "You got me."

They led their horses to the holding pen. Beck was the tenth competitor. No matter the rodeo, some cowboys were silent, in their heads or on their phones, while others were chatty—fully of verbal swagger. Beck used his time to catch up with friends between events, not during, but he wasn't nearly as unapproachable as Bowen, who would rarely speak unless necessary once the rodeo had started. He was often more relaxed at Copper Mountain Rodeo, but even that wasn't saying much.

Bodhi had always been a damn master of ceremonies with the comments and the shout-outs, but not today. Bodhi stood next to his horse, Cash—named after his favorite country music singer—and stared hard at the ground, every line in his body rigid, his jaw clenched, eyes shuttered.

"You okay?" Beck asked.

No answer.

"Bodhi?"

"Never better," Bodhi lied. No smile.

"What's going on?" A wave of concern washed over Beck.

"Nothing." Bodhi flashed a parody of a smile. "I'm the one who cares about nothing and no one, so I'm blessed with no worries." His voice was hard, eyes harder.

Beck stared at his cousin, trying to think of a way to voice his concern, to break through the suddenly heavily fortified wall.

"Are you mad I got back together with Ash?" he asked in disbelief.

"Congratulations," Bodhi said flatly, his eyes lit with some repressed emotion Beck couldn't begin to understand. He stared helplessly at his cousin. Bodhi had always liked

Ash. They'd been in all the advanced classes together in high school and in college they'd both been pre-med track. They often studied together.

He waited for Bodhi to say more. He always had to have the last say…well, until today with only the tense energy radiating off him like a blast of heat.

"You were the one who kept telling me I should marry her. That I'd never meet another woman her equal."

"You won't."

"Bodhi, you aren't really taking the Rodeo Bride Game seriously, are you?" he demanded.

"Why wouldn't I? You are."

"I'm not. I'm with Ash. I've always been with Ash." For a moment he almost shared his news, but the new hardness in Bodhi kept his confession locked down. "You're not really going to bring Nico home and get down on one knee and propose to a girl you've known a week. Granddad won't fall for that."

"We'll see. You got something special planned for Ash?"

"We'll see." He threw Bodhi's words back in his face.

"If you propose, you have to go through with it."

Beck's jaw clenched tight. "That's why I'm not acting so irreverent about marriage." Bodhi questioning his commitment was rich. "But yes. I intend to marry Ash. Soon as I can." He didn't mean to make it sound like a taunt, but it did.

"Good," Bodhi said, his voice short, unconcerned. "I'll be proposing at the Bash too. I don't back down, and I'll never walk away from ensuring Granddad's happiness at the ranch."

Beck snorted. "You. Public proposal that lights up Granddad's imagination. Right."

"Think I can't stick it?" Bodhi demanded.

"You won't," Beck said confidently. Bodhi didn't do relationships except one-night horizontal ones. "You'd never follow through. Never. Ever."

"You know me, cuz." Bodhi swung himself up on Cash.

Beck jumped. He hadn't been paying attention to the lineup at all and, he was up in three competitors. He'd been so caught up in Bodhi's gaming that he'd lost his focus. Just like at the Panhandle rodeo.

"When I play, I play to win." He looked down at Beck. "Get your head in the game, Beckett," Bodhi taunted. "Ash is going to want you in one piece when you drop down on one knee and confess undying love and devotion."

Beck wanted to tell Bodhi to cut the machismo because he wasn't playing, but the idea of beating Bodhi at his own game appealed in a way he knew it shouldn't. Old habits die hard, he thought ruefully.

"Keep your eye on the competition because I'm not going down without one hell of a fight, cuz," Bodhi said.

BECK WAS IN the zone. Game on. He sat atop Raider, perfectly balanced, waiting for the string to be released.

Raider danced sideways, showing off, tossing his dark mane that Beck had brushed until it gleamed but, always a pro, Raider settled quickly, muscles bunched in anticipation. Beck didn't have to look to know Bodhi would be ready. He might joke around, but no one worked harder.

The antsy steer was loaded into the chute, and Beck drew in a deep breath. Waited behind the barrier. He saw a blur of white and brown and the string broke, popping the barrier down. Raider burst out at a full gallop. Bodhi and Cash kept pressure on the steer, and Beck was practically parallel to the steer before he released a breath. He dropped, arm straddling the steer, both hands gripped the horns, his legs were out straight but not locked, and as his boots caught dirt, he shifted his weight, twisted and hauled the steer over and down. The steer's legs were up even as Beck's butt hit the dirt.

He released the steer, which rolled back up, shook its head and ran off. Beck popped up out of the dirt and sawdust. Bodhi had Raider's reins and he looked at the clock before trotting over to meet him. Beck tipped his hat and waved. Ashni was on her feet waving a cute black straw cowboy hat and cheering. He waved at her and then strode out of the arena.

"Three point nine seconds in the prelim. Damn, you're on fire. You should at least let the other cowboys think they've got a shot." Bodhi laughed as he dismounted. He slapped Beck on his back. "Off to see a girl. See you round."

Beck stared at Bodhi as he led Cash away, swagger in

every step, but for the first time, Bodhi didn't flirt with any of the rodeo queens he passed, who were waiting, glittering and glamorous after their ride through the arena, to kick off the rodeo. Bodhi tipped his hat and murmured, "Ladies," and kept on moving.

His friend Boone Telford joined Beck and walked with him and Raider back to the livestock holding area. "I rodeoed for seven years and didn't get but a handful of scores below four."

"Luck was on my side," Beck said, fist-bumping and shoulder-checking Boone. It was true, but he also trained and trained and trained some more. And kept his body in competitive athletic shape. "Bodhi really cranks the pressure when he's the hazer."

"He's good. Looking forward to watching him and Bowen vie for the higher score when the bull riding starts. And I hope your bulldogging score doesn't match your steer wrestling."

"Still working on your stand-up, I see," Beck mused as he rubbed down Raider. "Keep at it—you're still not funny."

He saw Bodhi in a stall on the other side, taking care of Cash and listening while Nico, perched on the gate, her hair a lava flow that seemed to have a life of its own, chatted.

"I'll keep that in mind," Boone said. "I was hoping to catch you today to invite you and Ashni to dinner next week if you're still planning on staying the extra week like you normally do. I wanted to show you my rodeo school plans so you've got something to think about as you finish off your season."

"Thanks, Boone, I'd like to see what you've got going so far and look over your business plan if you have one."

"Oh, I have one. My dad is not about winging anything. He brought his family's ranch back from near bankruptcy and has tripled its size over the years, buying back land his father had been forced to sell."

"I'll check with Ash what night works best. I'm not sure what, if anything I have to offer, but, yeah, I'd love to talk about what your program would need. Thanks for thinking of me."

Maybe this could be his first step in life after the rodeo. He still hoped to work the Three Tree Ranch with his granddad, of course. It had been his lifelong dream. In his dream, his cousins had also been with him, but they'd always known that they'd have to bring money to invest in the ranch and have something else to support themselves. He'd been thinking about setting up a woodworking shop—making furniture, cabinets—but maybe working with Boone could provide some income while he got established. With a baby on the way, he'd need to be prepared to provide.

Boone seemed pleased. Congratulated him again on a stellar ride and said he was going to join his family to watch the roping events.

Beck brushed Raider's mane and tail again. Maybe he'd have enough time to sneak into the stands and find a few moments with Ash before his next event. What would she think about a rodeo school?

"Want to be a teacher?" he asked his horse.

Raider snorted and nudged at his pocket through the protective vest.

"Sneak," he said, fishing out the carrot. "I bet you'd be top of the class."

Chapter Thirteen

"I can help with that." Beck heard the familiar voice and his heart leapt.

Ashni took the tape from him, and her fingers were cool and gentle as she wrapped his left wrist and then laid a couple of pieces around his palm to help his gloves stick. He looked down at her silky dark head.

"You having a good day?" he asked softly.

She nodded. He put on his glove, and she wrapped the tape around his wrist. He tested for flexibility and tightness.

"Seems like you've done this before," he teased. "I'm looking forward to dancing with you at the steak dinner."

"Dancing with you is always my favorite part." She smiled up at him as she wrapped his right wrist.

There were lots of people around backstage at a rodeo—cowboys, staff, press, stock contractors and their employees, but she'd still made the moment feel intimate and playful as she teased him that there were lots of ways to dance, and she loved each one. But this year he had something special planned, and he very much hoped that was her favorite part of the night.

His stomach lurched both in excitement and with nerves.

"You gonna watch from here or from the stands?"

"From the stands. Your granddad is sitting with a friend of his—a Sam Wilder, who's become more and more of a recluse I've heard, and he disowned his daughter years and years ago, and now he's sitting there in the thick of his four grandsons he's refused to meet over the past few years since they all moved to Marietta. He's Sky's grandfather-in-law."

"Granddad must be thrilled. He and Sam go way back. Each year he drives out there to try to convince him to come to the Bash. Maybe this year he will." Beck crossed his fingers, awkward in the gloves as this was a newer pair, not yet broken in. "Glad you're sitting with him."

"I love him," Ash said. "But I wanted to spend time with you. I won't be doing this again, not often anyway," she said, tapping his other glove tightly.

"I thought you wanted to be done with all this." He kept his voice neutral, but he was curious. He'd given notice; he could change his mind, but he didn't think he would, not with the baby coming.

"I do. But the rodeo has been a large part of our life. I watched you compete since high school. I did most of your taping over the summers and helped when you were injured. It's bittersweet."

"For me too." He looked at her bare left hand and wished the ring was already glittering there. "I've got this last event today, and then I can sit with you and watch Bowen and Bodhi flop around like raggedly dolls."

He bent to kiss her.

"I don't flop. Pure ballet moves on the bull and the saddleless bronc," Bodhi said, pulling up short and grinning when he saw their posture. "Oh, am I interrupting?"

"You live to interrupt," Ash said, kissing Beck anyway and then she turned to face Bodhi. "And I was so polite earlier, not interrupting nor mentioning the romantic movie smooch I saw between you and an auburn-haired beauty down by the Marietta River while I was waiting in line at the Melt."

"I believe that is what's called mentioning," Bodhi said drily. "But what can I say?" He spread his arms wide. "The ladies love me."

"Ladies." Ash rolled her eyes. "You're losing your touch, Bodhi. I only saw one there today."

"A gentleman never kisses and tells," he shot back. They'd always been like this—verbal duelists. Ash was the only one Beck had seen best him.

"So that's why I know so much about your escapades," she mused.

Bodhi's eyes lit with delight at her comeback.

"Except this week. You've been awfully quiet." She studied him, tapping her finger against her lips.

Bodhi's smile fell, and Beck could feel his wall snap into place from here.

Ash looked at Beck, and her smile was like the sun. "Ride well and hard, cowboy," she said softly. Then she placed her hand against Bodhi's chest. He looked at her hand, then her, then at Beck with a WTF expression on his face.

Ash stood on tiptoe and whispered softly in his cousin's ear. Then her heels came down, but she was still looking up at him, her eyes searching his, her expression grave.

"I mean it, Bodhi. For reals."

His lips tightened, but he nodded, and Ash walked back down the aisle, like a queen on a red carpet with rose petals and subjects kneeling before her instead of dirt and sawdust and horses watching her with disinterest.

"What did she say?" Beck asked. Bodhi seemed lost.

"Didn't see a ring on her finger yet, cuz." Bodhi struggled to rally, and maybe because Beck had seen a crack in Bodhi's armor earlier or maybe because he was looking forward to his life-changing event tonight, Beck answered honestly. "Which means Bowen and I are still in the game."

Should he tell Bodhi he was out? No. Let him sweat. See how far he'd go.

"I'm waiting for a slightly more romantic, less smelly place."

"Really?" Bodhi's face was almost comical as a million expressions danced over it.

"Really what?" Bowen asked as he joined them.

"Damn," Bodhi said and clapped him hard on his shoulder. "Couldn't do better in...your wildest dreams. Congrats, cuz. Congrats."

For a moment, Beck thought he saw tears glitter in Bodhi's eyes, but Bodhi walked off, red fringe swinging from his very loud, very distinctive chaps. He didn't even acknowledge Bowen, and Beck figured he must have been mistaken.

Beck opened his mouth to tell Bowen he was going to propose to Ash tonight, but Bowen, true to form, was there before him.

"Time to saddle up, cowboy. I'll help with your gear," Bowen's eyes searched his. "Need you in one piece tonight. I promised Ashni."

SUMMER STORM WAS far too mild a name for the bronc he was about to drop down on.

"Should be called Class Five Hurricane," Bowen mused as if reading his mind. The bronc had been resistant since they'd approached. The stock contractor, Taryn Telford, was a Marietta local rancher, and bred some of the best bucking broncs on the Montana and Mountain rodeo circuit. He and his son Boone situated the horse in the chute with only one curse from Boone. Taryn grinned and slapped Beck on his back.

"Good luck, son. Hope to see you tonight at the steak dinner with only your pride injured."

"Oh, you'll see me in the winner's circle tomorrow," Beck shot back cheerfully.

"Keep the cocky, you'll need it." Taryn, who'd been an outstanding bull and bronc rider in his day, stepped down from the chute.

"He's not lying." Bowen tried for the second time with

the hook to get the saddle firmly cinched on. "Summer Storm is fierce and pissed and gearing to toss you head over boots into the dirt."

"Not going to happen." Beck checked his saddle. It was good and tight—not going to budge no matter what dance moves the bronc thought he had. He climbed up and over the top rung and breathed in deeply. He loved this part—the adrenaline, the smells of dirt and animal and leather, the feel of the crowd's anticipation, his cousins close, the rhythm of the rodeo and all the moving pieces—competitors, staff, fans, rodeo queens and his place in it all. He loved pitting his skills against the other cowboys and the animals.

How am I going to give this up?

The question wasn't surprising. He'd been asking himself that for the past couple of years. Maybe no cowboy was ever really ready. Maybe it was time that decided. Or a bad buck of fate, or maybe it was as simple as the cowboy standing at the top of a chute and telling himself that this would be the last time he dropped down on a bucking bronc or bull. And that the last time he climbed the fence after a ride to wave to the crowd acknowledging a solid performance or picked himself out of the dirt would be the first time he was stepping into a new future.

"You okay?" Bowen asked, his voice betraying a little worry.

Beck was not given to many moments of self-reflection. Usually he was eager to drop down and get a feel for the animal and let the animal get a feel for the cocky fool of a stranger who thought he could cage a ride.

He was better than good. His answer was to drop down, and as the bronc shifted uneasily under him, he set his feet in the stirrups, instinctively preparing to mark out. He wrapped his grip and tested it. Took one last breath, savoring the scents, the anticipation, the nerves, and the hope. He recentered himself high of the saddle, every muscle coiled and ready to go.

This was when he felt most alive.

But today, he finally accepted that there were so many ways to feel alive and thrive. So much more waited for him. Being a husband. A father. Building a life with Ash and their child. Discovering a new career and a new life and building it, brick by brick or with a hammer and nails.

Left hand high in the air, he gave the nod and was launched out into the arena to the cheers of what he considered his hometown crowd and the raucous blast of "Ridin' Dirty."

"THAT WAS FIRE!" Kane Wilder, once one of the top bull riders in the world, fist-bumped him and made room for Beck in the bleachers to watch the last event of the afternoon. "I never liked the saddle bronc. Too many things can go wrong. Too many rules."

"Like nothing can go wrong barebacking a top-tier bull," Beck answered.

"Not a thing," Kane said seriously, but his pale blue eyes that looked almost silver gleamed.

"That was a really good ride, Beck." Sky peered around her husband's body and that of her six-year-old daughter, Montana. "You did good in the roping too," she said somberly.

Beck choked.

"Good." Kane shook his head. "Way to knock a man off his horse, baby."

Sky smiled impishly, and Beck could see why she and Ashni had bonded so quickly. They had art in common, and she was fun and a bit irreverent. Plus, she was a mom, so Sky would be a good friend for her to have if they did move to Marietta permanently.

Sky sat with Ashni. They both wore sunglasses and straw hats and looked glamorous—almost like celebrities. He'd wanted to sit next to his girl, but he hadn't been sure he'd make it to the stands. Bodhi and Bowen were entered in bull riding, and usually Beck worked the chute with them, but because they rode on the pro tour, many of the local cowboys, who competed in the Montana circuit rodeo, had been eager to help out.

His granddad was deep in conversation with Sam Wilder—Beck didn't want to interrupt that. He wondered how all the Wilders were taking it—their grandfather finally acknowledging them after several years of trying to break the ice. How could a man throw out his own teen daughter when she'd been expecting? His own granddad had been such a constant in his life, a larger-than-life presence on what it meant to be a man, far more than his dad or his parade of stepdads. He didn't know who he'd be without his granddad's steady influence.

"Heard you're a woodworker."

"Beck Ballantyne," he introduced himself to one of Kane's other brothers who sat beside him, still, large and sculpted as hard as Copper Mountain's granite peak.

"Colt Wilder." His lips quirked as if something were funny, but then he went back to stone-faced. "I am not a part of the ranch or bull-breeding business except when they rope me in to help knock up cows. I do construction."

Beck waited for more, but Colt was silent after that. Colt's wife, Talon, introduced herself along with their son, Parker. She was also expecting—just starting to show. Her fingers lightly stroked the back of her husband's neck.

"Ashni came for dinner the other night and brought the guitar you'd made," Talon said.

Beck felt a burst of pleasure. Ashni had not been talking to him much at the time.

"Colt was impressed by the workmanship. He works with a team at Big Z's on construction projects during the late spring, summer and early fall, but the building season here is short so he does woodworking and builds tiny houses and modifies those Sprinter vans for people who want to live light or travel. He has a pretty massive shop he's built on the property." Her eyes shone with pride.

Colt looked down at his wife, and the tenderness that

fleeted across his face was as sweet as it was surprising, since Colt seemed to take stoic to a whole different level.

"I would love to see your shop and one of your conversions. Finding ways to increase storage sounds like a fun puzzle." Beck had loved to work with his hands since high school but had never had much opportunity as his mother hadn't allowed him to use their garage growing up and all of his traveling didn't allow him to buy or store too many tools. He only had a chance to work when he was at Three Tree Ranch.

"Been thinking about taking on a partner." Colt jolted Beck out of his reverie. "Not in a rush. But if you're interested, we can talk when you retire from the tour. Every man must eventually."

They exchanged phone numbers. Beck's heart ticked over with a combined sense of excitement and dread. He was really going to do it. Quit the tour. And having some work lined up would make the transition easier. Ashni might need some time to find a different job or she might want to volunteer at Harry's House, and he could build her an art studio on the ranch—if there was a ranch. Either way, he needed to be able to support them all.

Granddad was in his element in the family section surrounded by friends he'd known for decades.

Would he like Beck coming home for good, helping to take on more of the work, Ashni with him as his wife, a baby on the way? Would it be enough to sway him to stay, or was that hope selfish?

His granddad had batted away his attempts for a heart-to-heart all week by giving him lists of chores and generally being unavailable. After the rodeo—or after the Ballantyne Bash—he was definitely going to pin his granddad down. It was the best he could do for now so Beck settled in to watch the last event—and root his cousins on to get a spot in the finals tomorrow.

BOWEN'S RIDE WAS clean. Bodhi's was even better, but something went wrong in his dismount. Timing was always critical in rodeo—a tenth of a second mattered. Bodhi timed his jump and would have cleared the bull's massive head, but as he jumped, the bull, as if sensing the freedom both from the flank strap dropping and the bull rider launching, turned and reared so that its head clipped Bodhi's arm, which was not tucked in tight toward his body as usual.

Bodhi hit the dirt on both feet and ran. He cleared the arena and clamored up the railing even as the rodeo clowns surged forward to distract the bull. Bodhi, always a bit of a show-off, didn't wave to the crowd, which made Beck uneasy that his cousin had been injured. Bodhi dropped down on the other side.

"I'm going to go check on him." Beck was on his feet. Adrenaline could often get you up and out even with terrible injuries, but the grace period where pain didn't register didn't last long.

"You want me to come?" Ashni asked, starting to rise up still holding Sky's infant son in her arms.

"No, I'll text to let you know," he told her and lightly gripped his granddad's shoulder. He handed Ashni the keys to his truck. "Take Granddad home. I'll catch a ride with Bowen."

"So Ashni will be my date to the steak dinner." His granddad winked. "I'm claiming first dance. Make sure he gets an X-ray," he added, "even if he refuses."

Bodhi would definitely refuse.

"It's not that big of a deal, girls," Bodhi smirked at both Bowen and Beck.

"Girls?" Nico eyed him, her arms crossed and one boot kicked back against the wall of the backstage area. "You got an issue with *girls* or women?"

"Just one at the moment, darling." Bodhi smiled at her, but Beck could see pain edging over the cocky in his eyes. "I don't need an X-ray. It was just a friendly tap."

"Friendly, my ass," Bowen said. "I heard the crack."

"That was my brace." Bodhi held his left hand up.

"Why are you wearing a brace?" Bowen demanded. "What happened?"

"Stop acting like a mom—if any of us had moms like that," Bodhi said, his gaze quickly darting to Nico. She stared back at him, both challenge and an unspoken agreement in her steady gaze.

It was weird to see him so in sync with a woman. He and Ash had always been close—inside jokes between them and a love of science and weird medical trivia—but normally Bodhi's open, friendly charm with everyone only let people in skin-deep. He was private, even with his cousins.

"What happened?" Beck asked Nico. "Why's he wearing a brace?"

"I'll make sure he gets an X-ray today."

"How are you going to do that, darlin'?" Bodhi asked, his flirt back on, but a warning threaded his voice.

Nico wasn't intimidated.

"You taught me to rope." She winked. "Looks like I'll be roping me a cowboy instead of a fence post this time, *darlin'*."

Bodhi's eyes flared with shock, and Beck didn't bother to hide his laugh. Bowen coughed and choked.

"We'll take care of Cash," Beck said.

Bowen went one step further and reached into his duffel where he kept his supplies and a fairly extensive medical kit and pulled out a rope that, by the smell of it, he'd recently rosined.

"Have fun," Bowen said, handing Nico the rope. "The medical tent will likely have a portable machine, but the hospital's a stone's throw away."

"I am fine," Bodhi said.

"Don't be a baby." Nico walked right up to him, rope dangling from her fingers. "You taught me how to make a lasso, hotshot. Don't think I won't use it, and let's get a move on because you promised me a steak dinner and dancing under the stars."

"That I did."

"And I know promises aren't our thing this week, but I will hold you to that one."

"Two weeks."

"You'd better keep in tip-top shape then if you're going to try to persuade me to stay for two weeks."

"Our work here is done," Beck said heading out to take care of Cash.

"Hey, Beck, you get a date yet?" Bodhi called out.

"You'll just have to wait and see." Beck felt relieved by the back-and-forth between them, and he was especially pleased to see a woman stand up to Bodhi and flip him some manure that he definitely needed to keep his wild nature slightly in check.

"I got one," Bowen said. "Looks like it's game on."

"You boys are in trouble with this game." Nico laughed. "You know that, right?"

"Where's the fun in playing it safe?" Bodhi demanded. Then he took the rope out of her hand, draped it over her shoulders and reeled her in for a kiss.

Chapter Fourteen

Ashni laid her cheek against Beck's chest, her arms around his waist. She'd danced with Beck so many times in so many places, but the steak dinner in Marietta had always been her favorite. Tonight felt perfect. Blissful. Maybe it was cutting Beck loose that had made her realize how critical he was in her life. She knew they still had things to discuss—her job in Marietta, how and when they would see each other. But tonight she just wanted to have this moment with her man.

He'd made finals in all his events and oozed a warm, attentive playfulness that soothed her after such an emotionally tumultuous week. Bodhi was not too badly injured. And tomorrow morning, instead of helping out with last-minute preparations for the Ballantyne Bash, she was heading over to Sky's studio early before the pancake breakfast to discuss future volunteer teaching opportunities at Harry's House—including some science classes along with art.

Ashni was finally going to be able to build a home and a life she wanted. She still didn't know how Beck would fit in it, but she was optimistic they could make this work.

She let the music drift her away, feeling as if she and

Beck were in their own magical world. Although his heart seemed to be beating quicker than normal.

"Are you all right? You seem a little nervous. You weren't the one who got up on stage with Dylan Telford to sing a few songs," she teased. "Bowen did that. I'm still shocked he agreed."

She'd known Bowen played guitar and had a beautiful voice, but he rarely performed in public—and she, who loved open mics, would have loved to have had a partner to duet with over the past few years. She'd mostly stopped asking. The only times he'd sung with her had been at a few of the children's hospital visits.

"I'm happy," Beck said. "Just wishing I could have you alone."

She smiled. "You want to do another kind of dancing?"

"So much," he said. "But tonight. I want to go slow. I want to hold you in my arms and enjoy being together."

She'd been savoring the moment, but now that Beck had mentioned being alone, she'd be lying if she said she wasn't eager for some horizontal time with him. She'd heard women over the years discuss the merits of make-up sex, but until last night she'd never had anything to make up.

"Let's go back to my place," she said softly.

"Not the ranch?"

She heard the disappointment in his voice, but she wasn't quite ready for that—to go full-on family with Beck yet. She knew his mom and aunts would be there. His granddad and cousins. Beck would want to do a huge baby announcement and probably something high pressured like a way-too-public proposal. And she wouldn't know how to say no.

She wanted to be wanted for herself, not because of a baby, and she still hadn't found a way to let go of the hurt or find a way around that obstacle.

"My place is closer," she whispered seductively. "And more private."

And so, before the song ended, Beck was weaving her through the crowd at a fast clip while she laughed but pulled back. "My purse, and jacket and scarf," she reminded him.

"Stay put. Hold that thought," he ordered and sprinted back to their table, which had nearly cleared out, as many of the Wilders were dancing and Beck's mom and aunts seemed to be catching up with former school friends. Ben Ballantyne had headed home a few minutes ago.

She loved to watch Beck move. He easily dodged around couples heading on and off the makeshift dance floor. Heat stirred. He was sexy. Hers. And she had thought she could walk away and stay away from *that*.

They walked back to her studio, hand-in-hand. The comfortable quiet felt precious.

Beck opened her door, took off his hat, and then tapped the door shut with the soul of one boot. She dropped her jacket, scarf and purse on the coffee table and breathed Beck in. He was hers, and they had the entire night together—and one more week before he headed back on the road for at least another month. She knew he'd want to drive back and forth to see her, but it was draining on a cowboy, consuming energy, focus and money. She wanted Beck sharp so that he could compete at the level he needed to stay safe and achieve his dreams.

She just had to convince him that she would be fine on her own and that when he came to the ranch for his long break before the finals, she would be waiting for him. They would each have time to sort out their feelings and make plans.

"Ashni." He took both her hands in his, looking so serious, which was not how she wanted her magical evening to end at all.

She stepped into him, her hands moving up his body, pulling open the snaps of his shirt so that she could nibble on one of his nipples even as she soothed over it with her tongue.

Beck moaned low in his throat and she expertly kissed a sensuous path down his body. She undid his buckle and jeans and slid her hands inside his loosened pants and boxers to cup his ass, squeezing once she dropped to her knees and palmed his straining erection.

She circled his velvet tip, already leaking a little, with her thumb.

"Talk later," she ordered, her voice low in her throat. "Boots off now," she commanded. Then she leaned forward and slid her tongue across his tip. She dropped to her knees and, gaze on his heating one, she sucked him slowly into her mouth.

Beck growled, and his eyes fluttered before he rallied and followed her commands, managing to get out of his boots and shuck off his pressed black jeans and boxers, cursing the clothes a little. He rocked in and out of her a few times as his shirt fluttered to the floor.

"Ashni." He lightly stroked her hair as she used her lips and tongue and mouth to create a hot friction that made it seem like he'd lose control quickly.

"Baby, I'm not going to last if you don't…ahhhhh," he sighed as she varied her rhythm. She loved that she could still undo him—make him speechless and Gumby in bed. But he always rebounded fast and took charge so she had to savor her control while she had it, and then she'd be happy to lose it.

BECK COULD FEEL himself race toward climax, which had not been his intention. Not yet. He'd wanted to put on music, pop the cork on some sparkling cider he'd purchased and put in her fridge, light some candles, get down on his knee and propose to Ashni in a romantic way—telling her all the things he loved about her—the way she loved him was just one of many.

Driving her mindless in bed had been after the romantic proposal—after she said yes, shed a few tears, stared at the ring on her finger and then quivered in his arms while he'd lovingly and slowly undressed her and carried her to the bed.

While getting jumped, stripped and blown in the doorway had probably been on his fantasy list at some point, he'd imagined the end of this night quite differently, and yet her obvious enjoyment, devotion and the absolute focused skill of her hot mouth made any objection far beyond his level of self-control.

He let Ashni have her way, which ended up with him boneless, collapsing into the chair conveniently by the door and pulling her up on his lap so he could kiss her senseless and let the slow burn build up again.

They still didn't make it to the bed. He stripped off Ashni's dress and palmed her breasts and kissed and stroked her until she was wet and begging, but when he would have lifted her to carry her to the bed, she impaled herself and rode him. He let her tease him with the rhythm—fast and slow—and the squeeze of her muscles.

"I created a sex control freak," he murmured against her mouth.

She laughed. "You complaining?"

"Never."

"You taught me well."

"We taught each other."

"We have three weeks to make up for," she said, as if he needed any reminding.

"Oh yes," she bit out when he grabbed her hips, seizing control so that he could push up as he slammed her down. Ashni's fingers dug into his shoulders as he continued to pump, and she breathlessly urged him on. He changed the angle so that he could hit her sweet spot, and he felt the moment he tipped her over the edge.

Her feminine muscles gripped him while he continued to push into her over and over through her orgasm, until she collapsed against his chest, both of them hot, sweaty and spent. Their breath mingled and her hair was wild around them, a sexy, silky black cloud.

"I'm never moving," she murmured even as she pressed kisses against his throat.

"I got you, baby." He continued to hold her until he caught his breath and felt that his legs would hold them both.

Beck carried her to the bed, laid her reverently down and then sealed her body with his. She parted her legs so that she could cradle his body in hers.

"I missed you," he said, smoothing her hair out of her face. He should ask if she wanted for them to clean up. He'd often clean her with a warm, wet facecloth after lovemaking, which then ended in a second round, but now he just wanted to stay sealed to her—not let her escape through his carelessness. "I missed us."

"I missed us too," she admitted.

A shadow crossed her face.

"I have something for you," he said quickly. "I wanted to give it to you tonight. I had a slightly different plan for this evening."

She stroked her hands through his hair. It was shaggy. He needed a haircut, but he'd been too distracted to head to the barber, and Ashni had always wanted him to grow his hair a bit longer. Maybe he would. He turned his head to kiss one of her palms.

"Oh, Beck," she said, her voice full of regret.

In the act of extricating himself from her limbs that had tangled with his, he paused, his heart thudding so hard it hurt.

"You already got me a present."

"This isn't a present," he assured her, but when he lifted off her, she caught his hand. Brought his fingers to her lips and kissed each knuckle.

"Please don't give it to me. Not now," she said, her eyes swimming with tears.

"Why not?"

Unable to stand her pain even as his own engulfed him, he kissed the corners of her eyes, tasting her warm, salty tears.

"I just can't, Beck. Not now."

"But when? The baby…"

"That's just it." She held her finger against his mouth. "The baby. I don't want to marry because of the baby. I mean it."

"The baby is not the only reason," he said. "It just sped things up."

She pressed her lips together and then struggled to sit up. He shifted and helped her. Ash drew a silk, vividly patterned wrap on the opposite side of the bed to her and slipped it over her body.

"I don't feel that in here." She touched the Montana sapphire stone he'd given her. "In my heart. I still feel like the baby changed your mind about marrying me—not your feelings about me."

"Ash—"

"Please, Beck, don't make this harder. It kills me to hurt you. It does. And I'm hurting myself too, because I always imagined myself married to you."

"You will be."

She shook her head. "I wanted to marry you because I loved you and it was the next step, but the marriage was my destination—not just a part of my life journey, and I lost myself somewhere. I'm different. Something broke inside of me that night when I heard you talking to Bodhi. I know you explained. I don't want to beat you up about it. I even understand. And now I'm glad because it jolted me awake. I need to take more control of my life. I need to know I can stand on my own."

"Of course you can." He sat up fully and reached for her hands to hold them. "You're strong. Smart. Educated. Talented. You can achieve anything you want."

"What I want is to create a more independent, professional me before the baby comes. I don't want to just be your girlfriend and then your wife."

"You were never just my girlfriend." He couldn't believe the view she had of herself.

"That's how people saw me on the tour. Even though I worked in marketing, I was Beck Ballantyne's. Everything I did and had was because of you. Even my parents saw me and all I accomplished as just an extension of you and your world."

"You were my girl, but I was just as much your man."

"See, even the way you say it, it's not the same. Girl. I'm an adult. I need to feel that I have a life, a me outside of being a mother and your wife. I'm not saying never. I just want time to define myself. To be on my own."

"On your own? Why would you be on your own? We'll be together. The tour only—"

"I resigned my job," she interrupted him. "I've been finishing up some projects remotely. I'm staying in Marietta. I applied for a job with the public health department and got it. I start on Monday."

She uttered each sentence with a finality that sounded like the thud of a cowboy hitting the dirt and leaving him just as robbed of breath.

So much for communicating. He pulled away from her and stood up, uncaring of his nudity.

"You quit the tour and accepted a new job in a different town and didn't tell me?"

"I wanted to build my own life. I've never had that."

"Without me."

"Not forever," she said.

"How long?"

"I don't know. It's not an exact science."

"You're not going to be alone. You are carrying our child."

"The baby was unexpected."

"And changes everything. I quit the tour too. I'm planning to talk to Granddad about me moving to the ranch permanently to help out."

If he thought that would change anything, he was wrong.

"It's not a competition," she said scornfully. "You're quitting because of the baby?" She stood. "Don't bother. Pursue your career. Lots of cowboys on the tour have families. Rack up your points and endorsements while you can. It's always been your dream."

"You and the baby are my dream now."

Ash crossed her arms, unimpressed. "I am not marrying a man who only is interested in marrying me because we had an oops."

"Don't say that."

"Oops."

"Your dad will freeeeeak if we don't get married. My granddad will kick my ass all the way out of Montana. You wanted a big wedding—a blend of East and West. We don't have a lot of time to make that happen before the baby. We could get married by a judge and then do the big wedding and party after the baby comes when you're feeling well again."

He could not shut himself up. He heard himself talking and talking, and he knew, absolutely, that this was not working. The most important moment of his life, and he was blowing it. Big-time.

"We've been over this," Ashni said impatiently. "I'm not

marrying you because of the baby."

"And again, just to be clear, I am still not *not* being married to my child's mother. What kind of a man would that make me? I would despise that man."

"It's not about you."

"What am I supposed to say to our child when they ask why their mom and dad aren't married? How do you plan to explain it—that you said no because you want to be your own woman? I don't keep you in a cage. I don't have a leash. If we don't marry, all those things your parents thought about me will come true."

"Are you listening to yourself?"

He wished he hadn't been.

"None of what you're saying is about how you feel about me, about me being your wife and you being my husband. None of it was about how you want to build a life with me. All of it was about how other people will perceive you if you don't marry a woman you accidentally knocked up. And you're not quitting the tour to build a life with me. You're doing it because of the baby."

"The baby is a game changer," he admitted and then wished he hadn't.

"Everything's a game to you."

"This is not a game, and I am not playing." He picked up his clothes and dressed quickly and before he uttered any of the words that were screaming around in his head, he walked out, barely resisting the urge to slam the door.

"THIS IS DUMB," Ashni muttered walking along the outside perimeter of the steak dinner and searching for Beck. The crowds had thinned slightly. Most couples and groups had finished eating or were indulging in dessert and still sitting at the tables chatting, drinking iced tea and tapping a finger or hand to the band's beat.

She'd changed back into her dress and added a long swing cardigan and a scarf for warmth to stave off the night breeze that rolled down Copper Mountain. She wished she'd added leggings as the hay from the bales that marked off the footprint of the event kept scratching her as she walked.

Funny. Hay never used to bother her. She and Beck had gotten up close and intimate in hay over the years. Just the smell of it often evoked pleasant memories.

But now it was irritating—just like everything else. Not much used to bother her. But this year it was like all the things she'd brushed off, laughed off or hadn't even thought about had hit home. Was it because she was turning thirty next birthday? Was it because Reeva had met a man and fallen deeply in love and married in the same year? Was it because her mom and dad had sat her down prior to the start of the wedding festivities and told her she was wasting her life and her education and reproductive years? Yes, her father had said that. Her cheeks heated with shame. If he only knew!

But no. She hadn't told her parents that she was expecting or settling down in Marietta. What would disappoint them more—that she wouldn't come home to Denver or that she'd gotten pregnant before marriage? And did her parents' and their massive social groups' opinion matter that much to her? Was she as focused on public opinion as she'd accused Beck of being?

Ashni would have scoffed at that concept. It's not like her parents had ever approved of Beck in the first place. The ranch and rodeo had made them nervous, and as the relationship progressed, they'd worried she'd lose sight of her goals.

And she had.

But that was her fault—not Beck's. He was right. This year she'd just been so dissatisfied, but she'd said nothing. How could he be her partner when she didn't share the bad as well as the good?

All she knew now was that she wanted to have purpose. Her own identity. Would working at the public health department and teaching art and science classes on the weekends or after school provide it? Would being a mother provide it? She stopped in her tracks. Her hand drifted down to flatten over her abdomen. Life grew there. She was responsible for another human.

"And I have to get my head on straight before you arrive, mister."

A boy. She was convinced she was having a boy. And a boy would want and need a father. She'd created the rift with

Beck so she could get some breathing room. Now she needed to stop panicking that she wasn't strong enough and start bridging the gap.

Ashni finished rounding the park without seeing Beck. It had probably been a long shot. If he were mad, he'd probably take a drive to cool down. Head out to his favorite part of the ranch, Plum Hill, and sit somewhere and take in the view.

"Hey, I thought you left with Beck," Sky, walking with her husband off the dance floor spotted her and called out.

Ashni hesitated. She didn't feel fit for company.

"We did." She blushed. "But then I…we…I—"

"Baby." Kane kissed his wife and pulled her into his arms. "I'll wait for you at the table. You're not too tired?"

"No, I feel good." Sky sparkled with happiness. She brushed her knuckles along her husband's cheek. "Thank you."

Then she turned to Ashni as her husband tipped his hat to them both and walked off.

"What happened?"

"It's me," Ashni confessed. "I love him. I want to be with him. But I don't trust him." The confession whooshed out of her with a rush of clarity, and she sat down abruptly.

"Trust?" Sky echoed.

"I don't trust his feelings for me," she clarified.

"He loves you," Sky said. "You've been together since high school. And I saw him with you today at the rodeo—the way he looks at you when you're speaking—total attention. The way he watches out for you—bringing you snacks, helping you with your scarf or coat, the way he watches you—that's love. Is he upset about the baby?"

"He hopped right on board with the baby," Ashni said glumly. "Tonight he tried to propose—*again*, and he said he's quitting the tour."

"And that's bad?" Sky seemed to be trying to keep her voice and expression neutral, but she failed.

Ashni sighed. Beck thought she was being unreasonable. Her new friend thought so too although she was too polite to come out and say anything. What would Reeva think? No way would she bother Reeva on her honeymoon for a late-night heart-to-miserable-heart.

"I want him to love me for me," she admitted. "He didn't propose to me after years of being together and loving—" she used air quotes "—each other or quit the tour until the baby. I feel like I'm not enough."

There. She'd said it. Out in the open.

Sky stared at her, compassion in every expression that skidded across her expressive eyes, and the slim lines of her body. Sky leaned forward and pulled her into a fierce hug.

"Let's take a walk," she said. "I want to tell you about me and Kane."

"Kane adores you. His eyes and whole face light up when you enter a room. Every time you speak, he stops what he's doing and listens." Ashni sighed.

"That was my point about Beck earlier," Sky said wryly, sliding her arm through Ashni's and walking slowly around the perimeter of the tables. "Like you, I knew Kane when I was a kid. He was my brother's best friend. My parents weren't very warm for a lot of reasons I'll tell you about another time, but I worshipped my brother, who was older by about four years. He let me tag along with him and Kane a lot, and how many twelve-year-old boys can you say that about? Kane was always nice to me, but one day, I was watching them get ready to go swimming and Kane was wearing a pair of my brother's board shorts, and he was staring at the pool, and he was so still and angry-looking, hungry, and something inside me just cracked open."

"Puberty is the downfall of many women," Ashni said, remembering the exact moment her friendship with Beck suddenly became something else—mind-blowing, disturbing and thrilling.

"Anyway. I crushed hard and forever and then one year after my brother had died and I was in my first year of college and Kane was on the tour, he stopped by to see me and well, I ended up spending the summer with him on the tour. I knew it was temporary. He was clear that he hopefully would head into the finals while I would go back to the school in the fall. Of course for me, I was in over my head in love, but didn't dare tell him. I was never brave enough to ask him about his feelings for me or if we could see each other again. And I didn't dare tell him that I loved him. He felt like my whole world. I would have given up school for him and followed him on the tour in a heartbeat." She snapped her fingers.

Ashni saw where this was going. She'd felt the same. Her dad and mom had pushed medical school since she was in kindergarten. Talked about it like it was a done deal, and while she'd excelled in science and enjoyed it, she found her happy place with dancing and art and theater. And Beck. She hadn't wanted to break up or spend years apart in four more years of school and another four or five in residency. It hadn't seemed worth it, and she still had no regrets.

"What changed your mind? Did he come after you?" Ashni could picture it. The images in her mind practically had a swelling soundtrack.

"No. Not for years."

"What?" Ashni couldn't imagine Kane walking away from anything or anyone he wanted.

"I was afraid. I wanted him to do all the heavy lifting. I was so insecure because of my family." Sky waved that all away. "My point is, if I had told Kane that I loved him, that I wanted to stay with him, he would have agreed. He felt the same way, but he didn't want to interfere with my education. So he said nothing and dropped me off with a smile at the airport and missed me like crazy, and I missed him more. I didn't tell him I was expecting Montana. At least you didn't make that dumb mistake. He missed out on three years of her life."

They stopped walking. Sky looked toward the table where so many of her family members were sitting and chatting. As if magnetically aware of his wife, Kane Wilder stopped talking and looked at her. He smiled, and she smiled back, and Ashni felt as if she were on a different planet from them.

Beck had always made her feel that way—that they were alone and connected in their own world.

"Even when he tried to visit after a couple of months, I was too proud and pushed him away. I didn't want him to marry me out of guilt or responsibility about Montana."

"Exactly," Ashni said.

"But emotions aren't set in stone," Sky said. "Even if he had married me because of the baby, we would have grown together or maybe apart. But by me being afraid, Montana missed out on three years with her daddy, and he missed out on her birth and infancy. I can't give that back to him no matter how many kids we have."

The lump of guilt in Ashni's throat was big and bumpy as a toad.

"When he learned about Montana, he was so angry and so hurt. I did that to him and to our child because of my insecurities and fears."

Ashni frowned. "But you're both happy."

"Blissful. Montana now has a mom and dad, siblings and a huge extended family. Your child will have that with Beck and his family. And you'll have that with Beck."

"So you think I should just agree and marry him and not worry about the why of it?"

"I think you should open your heart," Sky said cautiously. "Give Beck and the idea of marriage a chance."

"I've been feeling so proud of myself for asserting more

independence and building a new life," Ashni admitted.

"You can create a life you are happy in. You can work and create and volunteer and be a mom and a wife. I do all of that. Do you want to be alone to prove a point?"

Ashni sucked in a deep breath. Put like that, the answer was no. No. No. No.

"Relationships are organic. They change. You don't know what your relationship will grow into once the baby arrives and you and Beck marry and settle in Marietta. And marriage is just the start of your life together. It's not a destination."

"I feel like I just gave and gave until I had nothing left," Ashni said sadly. Although that wasn't entirely true either. She hadn't asked Beck for anything in return.

"So you've made a move to change," Sky said, turning them back toward her family. "Now you need to let Beck make his move to change with you."

"And maybe we'll meet somewhere in the middle," Ashni mused, feeling a leap of hope that she hadn't felt in a long time.

Chapter Fifteen

Beck hadn't had much of an appetite for the pancakes, but his mom and aunts and granddad had wanted to come to the annual rodeo pancake breakfast, which had surprised him. So he'd played dutiful son and grandson. He'd brought the plates of pancakes and bacon to the table. He also brought everyone a large drip coffee before he finally sat down to stare at his stack, glistening with butter and dripping with syrup.

His stomach revolted, but his granddad dug enthusiastically into the food and happily talked about the Bash tonight. His mom and aunts chatted—all the details were finished, and they were going to watch the finals, a fact that Beck found hard to believe, but he kept that thought, like everything else in his life, locked up tight.

He stared across the park with the sea of people and the tables with blue tablecloths and families eating, laughing, so much life.

Bowen and Bodhi arrived and lined up—Langston and Nico chatting like old friends.

"No Ashni this morning?" his mom asked.

"No."

He didn't have an excuse. He waited for his mom to weigh in with some dismissive remark.

"What's wrong?" And for once, heavy judgment didn't weigh down her question.

Everything. Nothing. Both words vied for an exit strategy from his mouth, but instead he pushed his plate away. The coffee he could maybe keep down.

"She wants to break up," he admitted. "She's angry I waited so long to ask her to marry me."

"Why did you wait? It's not like you didn't adore that girl from the moment you met her." His mom, her coffee cup halfway to her lips, paused and looked at him. Some of what he felt must have been in her expression. "Ah. Yes. I can imagine my parade of husbands was hardly a conducive example to wedded bliss." She rolled her eyes. "At least I was persistently and consistent in my disasters." She grimaced, and it was the most self-aware moment from his high-powered, driven mother that Beck could remember.

"Do you want to marry her?"

"Yes."

"So what's the problem?"

And that was the crux of it. He didn't know. And his mom with four marriages under her belt was hardly the person to ask for advice. Should he tell her about the baby? No. Not now. The baby should be celebrated. Not admitted to like some guilty secret. And not when he had no idea where he stood with Ash. He knew he had to fight for her. He just didn't know how, and if he let himself play out the worst-case scenario, he saw himself in front of a judge begging for partial custody of his own child, and he just couldn't let his mind go there. He'd be destroyed.

"Women are complicated," his mom mused, much to Beck's growing astonishment. She'd always dismissed his problems with a wave of her hand because she was too busy. His problems were too small, beneath her notice. She'd snap out a solution and move on.

"They want love. They want romance. They want to be taken outside of themselves. Transformed into someone new by love. They want a fantasy that they can float around in where they are loved and cherished and everything glows."

Beck stared at his mom. That didn't sound like Ashni at all.

"At least I was like that," his mom said. "I wanted this mirage, but life is hard and reality cold and the mirage would always implode, and I was myself again. Alone."

"Was that so bad to be yourself?"

"It must have been. I lost each one of my husbands. Drove them right out the door," his mom admitted. "Drove you out too."

That was true, but Beck now saw it from his mom's perspective—wanting something that the other person was unable or unwilling to give.

"You pushed so hard," he said. "I was never good enough."

"You were always better than good enough," his mom said. "I just wanted you to be strong. Achieve your potential.

I was worried that you would settle because you didn't have a fire under your feet. Ashni has always looked at you as if you hung the stars and moon for her—Dad used to say that about our mom. That she thought he decorated the sky for her, and he would have if he could. He was the most loving man I ever met." She smiled at her father. "I never found another man even close. You're like that. Ashni is very blessed. I hope she realizes that."

Beck blinked. His mom had never complimented him that he could remember. Ever. And she'd never mentioned her parents' marriage.

"Maybe Ashni just found Mr. Right too soon so she doesn't know what she has. You should show her. Fight for her."

Beck sipped his coffee for a few more moments. "I intend to," he said. "Just trying to think of a strategy."

"Make it a game." His mother didn't look at him, but her lips curved in a smile. "You and your cousins always excel at games. My sisters and I are still always trying to one-up each other. And Dad doesn't stand on the sidelines," she said affectionately.

"Ugh, no," he groaned. If his mom only knew. "Making a game out of winning her back is the last thing Ashni needs."

"I don't know, she's fairly competitive," his mom said. "Speak of the devil."

"Hey, Beck." Ashni's voice jump-started his heart. "Do you have a moment?"

Nothing like opening up your heart in front of the town. Ashni switched her weight from side to side and gripped her fingers together as she stood behind Beck at the pancake breakfast. So many of the tables were already full, and the Daughters of Montana volunteers were still cooking pancakes and bacon on massive griddles. She wanted to flee, but she'd screwed up, and she had to own it, and she had to confess her feelings and her fears before Beck competed today so his head would be clear.

"Sure." He popped to his feet, sending relief washing through her.

He looked a little haggard, as if he'd slept as poorly as she had.

"Hi." Ashni waved as Beck's mom and his aunts smiled and greeted her. His granddad patted the empty place next to him and told Beck to go get her a plate.

"I will, Granddad, but we're going to take a walk first." He lightly wrapped his arm around her and steered her through the crowd.

"Do you want me to get you some pancakes?"

She was having a hard enough time with this. Eating something would definitely be a disaster for her queasy stomach.

"I want to apologize," she said in a rush as they headed away from the crowds and around to the other side of the courthouse so that they weren't on the path leading to the fairgrounds.

"You don't..."

"I do." She placed her hand on his chest. His heartbeat was steady and that gave her courage. "I've been all over the map this week emotionally."

Massive understatement.

"A lot of changes," Beck said—accepting, steadying like he always was. Her throat clogged with emotion and her eyes pricked.

"You're right. I should have confronted you when I was hurt. I should have shared that I was tired of touring. I should have insisted we keep the dog. I should have told you about the job offer. So many mistakes to keep the peace."

"Water under the bridge," he said.

"No. Because I was hurt and angry but didn't do anything about it. I let it fester, and I closed off. But really, it started before that. You re-upped for the tour without discussing it with me, and instead of calling you on it and telling you how I felt, I started shutting myself off from you."

"I felt that. All year I felt it," Beck admitted. "I didn't know what to do, and I didn't ask you what was wrong."

"I've been blaming you for our lack of communication," Ashni said. "But it's been me too, and I think I have a bigger role to play because I recognized what was happening, and I let it. I felt self-righteous about it, and I think Reeva's wedding, when you didn't come with me, just made all of my resentment blow up. I felt you valued the rodeo and your points more than me."

"Ash," he said. "No."

She dragged in a deep breath. "It was easier to blame you for my unhappiness instead of myself."

She held on to his hands that were so large and warm and callused from hard work. They always steadied her. She gazed into his beloved sky-blue eyes.

"I realized last night that I was acting like my mother. She's so passive sometimes. She won't share her hurts or anger or disappointments and instead withdraws and then just strikes fast and retreats like an eel. It maddened me when I was a teenager, and I swore that I would be stronger than that—that I would be emotionally honest with myself and with you and I would be an active participant in my life, and yet when I hit my first hurdle really, I did the same thing—shut you out and looked to place the blame on someone else. I'm sorry, Beck. So very sorry. You deserve better."

He rubbed her chilled hands in his. "It's not all on you, Ash," Beck said. "I can see why you thought I valued the rodeo more than you. I did get obsessive about the points, always comparing myself to my cousins. And I didn't come to you to talk about my worries about Bodhi this year. And I never confessed how much my mom and her string of failed marriages bothered me. Or how her endless criticisms just kept flaying pieces off of me. I pretended nothing hurt when it did. I didn't want to look weak to you because you always looked at me with stars in your eyes, and I loved that. I needed that."

"I still do," she said shakily.

"Ash." He pulled her into his embrace, and he felt so good—so warm and strong and Beck that she just clung to him. "We've both made mistakes, but we can learn from them. Communicate better."

"We'll need to," she mumbled against his so strong chest. "That's why I didn't tell you about the job at the public health department in Crawford County. I was afraid you'd talk me out of it, and I really, really needed a change and to feel like I was doing something for myself, not just always have your goals as a top priority."

"We can share our goals and support each other." He made it sound so simple, and maybe it was. She just had to stand up for herself and what she wanted more. Not defer and resent as her mother had so often done.

"Teaching at Harry's House this week has made me realize how much I want to work with kids and have art in my life as well. I do want to work at the public health department. That's important to me, but I also want to have time for my own art and to volunteer at Harry's House."

"I want you to have those things. That's why I quit the tour, and it wasn't just because of the baby," he said. "Look." He scrolled through his phone and showed her the sent email to the tour.

"The date." Her breath caught. "That was before I told you about the baby," she said, her heart feeling like a balloon that had been released.

"And before I knew you'd taken a job here. I just wanted to make the commitment to you, to us, that we would start a new phase in our lives. And that I would support you in your dreams just as you supported me."

"You're sure you're ready, even if Bodhi and Bowen don't quit?"

"I'm ready," he said. "I won't lie and say I won't miss parts of the rodeo. I will. I love competing. I love the camaraderie, but I'm ready to start something new." He pulled her into his embrace. "I'm ready for all of it Ash—a home, an art studio for you and a woodworking shop for me and our baby and when you're ready and if you'll have me, marriage. We can have it all, Ashni. Everything we've ever wanted. Everything." His voice took on a deep significance.

"THIS IS GOING to be the best Ballantyne Bash ever," Ashni sang out. She'd watched the finals with Beck's family, but she'd kept her pregnancy a secret. Beck wanted to make the announcement together tonight, and she suspected that he'd probably produce a ring at some point in the evening.

Her reluctance to get engaged seemed more like a bad dream that had faded in the daylight. Beck loved her. She loved him. Sure, the baby might have inspired him to propose, but after talking to Sky last night and confessing her feelings to Beck this morning, she felt more confident. This was a new step they were both taking. And she'd have some time. Her new job started Monday, and in a week, Beck would leave for the last leg of the tour, giving her a few weeks to be on her own and settle into a new normal. She didn't want to move onto the ranch without him, and he hadn't pushed it. A pleasant surprise. She liked the studio, and she'd never had time to live on her own. She'd gone from her parents' home to a college dorm, to living with Beck in an apartment or his rig.

Beck went back to the truck to bring in another keg of beer, and she hurried ahead into the log cabin on Plum Tree Hill where they were staging salads and desserts. She had two boxes of rodeo-themed cookies she had ordered from the Copper Mountain Gingerbread and Dessert Company and a large collection of dark and milk chocolate mini cowboy boots from Sage's.

She'd begun to put the cookies on a platter when the tall, gorgeous woman with auburn hair she'd seen with Bodhi a few times this week sauntered in and offered to help. Ashni was eager to meet her. Bodhi rarely hung out with the same woman twice. Had someone finally captured his heart?

"Nico Steel," she said. "You've been having fun with Beck this week," she observed.

That was one way of putting it.

Nico stole a cookie and took a bite then she smiled. "These are delicious."

A vaguely familiar blonde walked in.

"This is Langston," Nico said. "She's our competition although it's all friendly from our end. We've become friends when we were roped into helping set up and decorate for the bash, but Beck's been keeping you under wraps."

"I was teaching an art class," Ash said, hoping she wasn't staring too hard at Nico. She'd never seen Bodhi take an interest in another woman longer than a one-night stand.

"Hey, Ashni," Langston smiled and also grabbed a cookie from the plate Ashni still held. "Good to see you. Last time I think was when you'd just graduated high school and you came for a visit with Beck."

"That is a blast from the past," Ashni said, charmed that both Bodhi and Bowen had dates for the bash for once. Usually they were just about granddad and the ranch when they were home.

Maybe they too were getting the urge to settle down.

"What did Beck offer you?" Langston asked startling her out of her musings about Beck's cousins' potential romantic lives.

"What?"

"Other than the obvious." Nico laughed.

"What did you get out of the game?" Langston asked. "Bowen did a favor for me with my ex. Nico's new in town and Bodhi's been showing her around and teaching her how to live in the moment. Even though you've been together forever, Beck must have dangled something to play the game."

"What game?" Ashni felt her blood begin to chill. Bowen, Bodhi and Beck were forever challenging each other, making bets, playing games, keeping score. But what did this week have to do with a game?

"The Rodeo Bride Game." Nico rolled her eyes. "It was Bodhi's idea. And all three boys jumped in boots first. The goal is to encourage his granddad to stay on the ranch instead of sell it."

"Sell," Ashni echoed. Beck hadn't mentioned his granddad selling the ranch. She'd sat with Ben Ballantyne for two days at the rodeo, and he hadn't said a thing, the sly fox. He'd just told her to stay strong, and that he'd look out for her. This was going to be bad. Worse than bad.

Ashni put the plate of cookies down on the counter very slowly, trying to suck in some air.

"So they are playing a game," she questioned forcing calm in her voice when she wanted to scream. "What are the rules?"

"First one to get engaged, but it's got to be public in front of their granddad and moms and somehow dramatic or memorable. Granddad and moms are the judges," Langston said. "Surely, Beck told you all this."

"So what did Beck offer you?" Langston asked again.

"Marriage," Ash said, her throat dust dry.

"You don't have to spew the party line for us. We're all in on it."

"I wasn't," Ash admitted, but somehow it all made horrible sense. Beck's dogged persistence. Not for her. For the game. For the ranch.

"Hey, Ashni." Beck entered the kitchen, a huge smile plastered on his stupid, deceptive face.

"Beck, you jerk." Langston turned to him. "Didn't you tell her this was a game?" she demanded. "I thought since you guys have been together forever that she'd be in on it. Bowen assured me that all the women were in on the rules." Langston crossed her arms and glared.

"The Rodeo Bride Game." Ashni faced him. "That makes so much more sense than you suddenly deciding it was time to quit the tour and settle down. I'm out." She pushed past him. "You lose."

BECK STARED AT the open doorway where Ash had just disappeared. He heard the front door slam. He felt like everything was in slow motion and he had to move. Fast.

No. No. No. This could not be happening. She could not be running out on him again.

Beck sped out the door just as Bodhi headed in.

"Hey, have you seen Nico? It's showtime."

Beck shoved Bodhi out of his way and ran out into the night.

It was beautiful and macabre at once. The barn was ablaze with lights and a country band played inside. More than a few couples danced. Others were lined up at the various food trucks. Several bonfires were set up waiting to be lit. The stars blazed overhead. The fiddle player launched into a dreamy solo that made his heart ache. Everywhere people were laughing, talking, enjoying life. He heard his granddad laugh. But no Ash.

Would she run? Hide? Cry to Sky? Slash his tires? He didn't know. A week ago he would have said he knew her as well as he knew himself, but this was a new Ash. Stronger. Mysterious. Sexy and so appealing and part of his heart that he didn't want to live a day without her. But she still didn't trust him, and she was still running.

All the damn games over the years. The challenges. The bets. The dares. *When are you boys going to grow up?* He'd heard it from the moms. From Ash. From Granddad. And now this. The biggest game—the one with the most potential to hurt—only he hadn't been playing. Why couldn't she see that?

You never once backed down from a Ballantyne challenge.

He kept walking down Plum Hill until the party was far behind him. He looked out over the valley below. This used to be his favorite place growing up. Plum Tree Hill. The barn. The view. He'd felt like a king as he'd eat his fill of the ripe fruit in the summer and dream. He'd made love to Ashni the first time in the hayloft with the valley and the future spread out rich and verdant below them.

"Showtime," he heard Ash mock behind him. Relief coursed through him. She hadn't run away. She was confronting him. He could work with that.

"Don't you want to watch Bodhi and Bowen make fools of themselves with their big ta-daaaa! We're getting married?"

He didn't bother to turn around. He closed his eyes.

"You don't trust me."

"You don't talk to me," she parried.

He winced. It was true. But since she'd stopped running and was up in his face, he could give her the answers she needed even when it was hard.

"Why the game, Beck?"

"Bodhi's game. I thought it was stupid, but yes, for a moment I got caught up in the competition." He faced her. "But for me, it was real. My proposal was sincere. Our marriage when it happens will be forever. I tried to propose to you at your apartment, not in front of anyone. Just us. I ceded the field. You are everything to me, Ash. Baby or no baby. Ranch or no ranch."

She blew out a long breath. Then nothing. Silence. Finally. "Why?"

"You mean more to me than a future on the ranch or working with my cousins or the tour. I couldn't turn that into a game."

"Why a Rodeo Bride Game?" She came up behind him, and he could feel the brush of her body against his. Her arms slipped around his waist, and she rested her cheek against his back. "You were the only one in a relationship. It makes no sense for Bodhi to come up with that."

"We were worried about Granddad. He'd said he was thinking about selling the ranch, and it seemed so out of character. He's Mr. Marietta. He's still on so many ranching committees. The rodeo committee. He knows everyone. Still works every day. He has always taught us to love the land, to be stewards of the land, and we were worried that he was ill and not telling us. Or needed money, and he wouldn't ask. Or maybe that he was tired of being alone and running the ranch so he'd let the moms finally talk him into selling and moving to an assisted living facility near them in Denver."

He felt Ashni's fingers tighten on his. But he couldn't move his fingers to hold on to her.

"Keep talking."

"Bodhi thought that if one of us got engaged, Granddad would feel like the future of the ranch was assured."

"And Rodeo Brides was his answer?"

"Ironic since he's never dated the same woman twice as far as I know."

"But even with the game, you didn't swoop in, tell me about it and ask me to play?"

"No." Beck was adamant. "I know Bodhi and Bowen told the other women about the games, but you and I had problems, real problems that a quick conversation couldn't fix."

"I got lost somewhere," she said. "Just as I think you got lost."

"I was never lost, Ash." Beck covered her hands with his where they rested on the bucking bronc buckle he'd won today. "You are always my home."

He felt her lips press against his back, and he turned around to face her, ignoring the view he'd always coveted. "I just left them to play. But I am worried about Granddad, and he put me off each time I tried to talk to him. And

Bodhi and I fought. He went too far, and I punched him."

Ash tilted her head.

"But Three Tree Ranch and your granddad and cousins and Marietta are you, Beck. They define you. What you've always wanted in life."

He shook his head. "I define myself. And you define me as well. The life we make together will define me. I'll miss this if it's gone. Won't lie about that."

Ashni's eyes narrowed in calculation. They loved each other. What else was there to solve?

"Now that sounds more like my Beck," Ashni said musingly.

"I wanted to be yours from the first time I saw you. I never stopped wanting to be yours, but I can't marry a woman who doesn't trust me."

"I know."

"I can't marry a woman who thinks the worst of me and won't come to me with her concerns or problems or fears."

"I know." She sighed. "Good thing I'm not that woman anymore. Or I'm slowly trying to shed that passive role. I panicked in the kitchen, but once I got outside, I realized that you don't have a deceptive bone in your body. And also I'm tired of running. So I turned around, but you'd already hoofed it halfway back to the farmhouse, just like I tried to find you at the steak dinner afterward to apologize but ran into Sky who set me straight.

"This morning after you and I sorted through everything, I felt confident again. I was even thinking you'd propose tonight, and I'd say yes because I was confident in us again, but the game explanation threw me. It's like you and your cousins and the two women were all on a team, and I felt left out again, like I did that night you were talking to Bodhi about other women."

"I could never leave you out. You're a part of me," he admitted.

"For reals?" She widened her eyes and crossed them.

"Of course!" How could she joke at a time like this? His eyes burned looking at her. She was like a living flame—her dress a bright red and her yellow scarf draped around her graceful neck and trailed down her back. She looked like a goddess out of a Greek myth.

"You are mine, Beck Ballantyne." She pulled away enough to gaze up into his face. "Let's never shut each other out again."

"Never." He kissed the top of her head loving how her hair was so silky against his lips.

"So…" She looked up at him, the sparkle back in her eyes. "Do you want to really piss Bodhi off and go win this thing?"

"What?" He coughed out a laugh.

"It would serve him right. You got a ring, right?"

"I do," Bodhi admitted.

"So that's a yes? You agree to be my husband?"

"Hell yes."

"Let's go win the Rodeo Bride Game." She linked fingers with him, and she tugged on him until side by side they walked back up Plum Hill toward the party and his family and their future.

The End

Want more? Check out Cruz and Axel's story in *A Son for the Texas Cowboy*!

Join Tule Publishing's newsletter for more great reads and weekly deals!

If you enjoyed *The Cowboy Says I Do*, you'll love the next books in the…

Montana Rodeo Brides series

Book 1: *The Cowboy Says I Do*

Book 2: *The Cowboy's Challenge*
Coming September 2021!

Book 3: *Breaking the Cowboy's Rules*
Coming January 2022!

Available now at your favorite online retailer!

More books by Sinclair Jayne

The Texas Wolf Brothers series

Book 1: *A Son for the Texas Cowboy*

Book 2: *A Bride for the Texas Cowboy*

Book 3: *A Baby for the Texas Cowboy*

The Wilder Brothers series

Book 1: *Seducing the Bachelor*

Book 2: *Want Me, Cowboy*

Book 3: *The Christmas Challenge*

Book 4: *Cowboy Takes All*

Available now at your favorite online retailer!

About the Author

Sinclair Sawhney is a former journalist and middle school teacher who holds a BA in Political Science and K-8 teaching certificate from the University of California, Irvine and a MS in Education with an emphasis in teaching writing from the University of Washington. She has worked as Senior Editor with Tule Publishing for over seven years.

Writing as Sinclair Jayne she's published fifteen short contemporary romances with Tule Publishing with another four books being released in 2021. Married for over twenty-four years, she has two children, and when she isn't writing or editing, she and her husband, Deepak, are hosting wine tastings of their pinot noir and pinot noir rose at their vineyard Roshni, which is a Hindi word for light-filled, located in Oregon's Willamette Valley. Shaandaar!

Thank you for reading

The Cowboy Says I Do

If you enjoyed this book, you can find more from all our great authors at TulePublishing.com, or from your favorite online retailer.

Made in the USA
Las Vegas, NV
07 February 2022